"Yea ... dating, not intere

She ... ne door for her and Tom turned to greet her. She stopped dead in the doorway buying a minute to compose herself as she fiddled with her skirt.

The midnight-black tux hung on him like it had been custom-tailored. Maybe it had been. As manager of one of the newest and hottest properties in Vegas, he probably had any number of social black-tie events to attend. And she was wearing a dress from a secondhand shop. She automatically extended her hand as he held out his.

He tilted his head, regarding her as he drew her toward him, a smile deepening at the corner of his mouth. The green glint in his eyes that had once haunted her dreams was back.

"You look wonderful."

"So do you." She flushed and bit her lip. "I mean…"

"Yeah, it's a little like prom, isn't it?"

"I wish I had a camera to take a picture of you two kids." Magdalena leaned against the doorframe grinning. "But the photographers at the banquet should love you."

Damn, it wasn't fair how the tuxedo accentuated the dark line of his brows and lashes, the intensity of his eyes. The sun-brown of his hair seemed infused with gold tonight while the strong planes of his face, even the crook of his nose made an interesting juxtaposition against the simple elegance of his tux. She needed to get out of the apartment. Maybe on the street she could grab a breath of fresh air, fanning herself.

Praise for Nina Barrett

Four-heart rating from theromancestudio.com for *MARRIAGE MADE IN HAVEN*.

RETURN OF THE DIXIE DEB receives a Five-Star rating from Ashantay Peters, the Wild Rose Press author.

A Man to Waste Time On

by

Nina Barrett

Rachel – Enjoy!
Love, Jo

A Man to Waste Time On

Cover Art by *Debbie Taylor*

The Wild Rose Press, Inc.
PO Box 708
Adams Basin, NY 14410-0708
Visit us at www.thewildrosepress.com

Publishing History
First Crimson Rose Edition, 2015
Print ISBN 978-1-62830-756-6
Digital ISBN 978-1-62830-757-3

Published in the United States of America

Dedication

To Darla

Chapter One

"So, what do you think?"

Tom Marco's eyes were fixed on her, his jaw squaring. "I mean since…"

Yeah, she knew. Since he was "between girlfriends" as he had so eloquently put it, and she wasn't seeing anyone.

"I know it's short notice, the banquet coming up on Saturday."

It looked like a line of sweat was developing along his forehead despite the overhead-circulating fan sweeping the air with its artificial palm fronds. She watched him swallow as she tilted her head and studied him. He didn't look as if he were kidding. This dinner must be a big deal, one requiring a female on his arm even if it meant asking the kid sister of an old flame.

Tom's big hand gripped the handle of his cup. If she didn't give him an answer soon, another tea mug would find its way into the broken bits bin.

From the end of the marble counter, her business partner had stopped filling her tea infuser. She could feel Magdalena's dark eyes sending her covert signals—*say yes. Think of our bottom line. This could be huge—say yes, Cinna*!

"Yes."

"Yes?" His shoulders relaxed. He raised his cup and managed a sip.

"Sure." Cinna unclenched her jaw and tried for a smile.

The fact it was somewhat less than sincere apparently didn't register any more than her lack of enthusiasm.

"It's in the main ballroom at the convention center on Paradise Road beginning at seven. I'll get back with you before then. This is huge for the hotel. It's the first awards presentation since our grand re-opening."

"So will Gentleman Jim be going too?" Magdalena moved up beside her, adding her infuser to her cup. Her friend wasn't even bothering to pretend she hadn't been listening.

"No, he stays in nights at this point. He's comfortable in his apartment at the Imperial and going out at night is getting to be too much for him."

"Well, it's great that you're up for one of the major awards," Magdalena favored Tom with a broad smile as she stirred her tea with a spoon. The floral fragrance of her oolong drifted up.

"Yeah, it's an accomplishment. Even to be nominated is quite an achievement with all the competition we have out here. We appreciate the recognition."

"Cinna, the Las Vegas Hospitality Industry Awards are known as LasHos and they are a huge deal."

Behind the counter Magdalena's foot nudged hers—*get in the game, girl*. It was amazing how the ESP developed in college dorm rooms persisted over the years.

She found her voice.

"I haven't been inside the Imperial, but of course, I've been over that way. It looks wonderful, really impressive."

There, Magdalena, that showed she was trying, didn't it?

Tom seemed to relax. "It was Jim's idea to add the porte-cochere onto the front. Something to impress arriving guests. He also pushed adding the top two stories. It was part of our master plan to re-position the Imperial as a small, luxury hotel."

"Small only for Vegas. How many rooms do you have now?" Magdalena asked.

"Eight hundred. That's down from twelve hundred when it was the Outpost. Still some of the properties on the Strip offer thousands. During our renovation, we enlarged the rooms, updated our suites, and put more space in our restaurant and bar areas. When we open the West End next spring, we'll be able to offer nightly shows on the premises too."

"The old Outpost was rundown. You weren't here, Cinna, when it was in business." Magdalena shook her head.

"It was Jim McMasters who had the foresight to see what the property could be become if enough money and effort were invested," Tom said.

"From what I understand, you were the man with the plan though." Magdalena's voice dripped with more honey than their customers usually spooned on scones. "Can I top off your tea for you?"

"No, I need to get going." Tom took out his wallet and laid a bill on the counter. "Thanks again, Cinnamon."

"Here, let me get a travel mug for you. Cinna and I have been working on a new concoction and you can give us your opinion when you're in again."

Magdalena busied herself with the tea machine while Tom stood, fumbling for his keys.

The silence stretched on. *Snap to, Cinnamon*. She swallowed. Had Tom Marco actually asked her for a date?

"Everyone talks about how much better the whole Fremont Street area is now," she said. "Business seems to be on the upswing, more foot traffic and better sales."

"It's been a cooperative project working with the business community here, but I think it's paying off for everyone. Even if the Imperial's not in the black yet, we're heading that way. Jim has been the one spearheading it. For a man his age, it's a remarkable achievement. He's the one who sold it to the other investors."

"If you haven't been in Vegas for a few years, you wouldn't recognize this end of town." Magdalena added the cap to Tom's mug and slid it over to him. "The Outpost was a grind-house, low table minimums in their casino, cheap slots. That whole section of Ogden was nothing more than low rent hotels and strip joints. Now it's a whole different story."

"Sometime I'd like to show you both the Imperial. We're pretty proud of it." He took the mug Magdalena offered.

"I saw your casino chips when I was out the other day. They're really distinctive with those flags on them. Not like the others I've seen."

"Tom, we're working on getting those sample tea sets you asked for finished. Cinna, maybe you can take them over to the Imperial when we get them ready." Her partner smiled at her.

Thanks.

"That'll be great." Tom balanced his mug, newspaper, and keys and gave them both what looked like a grin of relief before he detoured around a pair of browsers at the pyramid of tea canisters she'd stacked earlier in the day.

Magdalena moved over to ring up a purchase of two tins of ginger with peach blend tea, diplomatically repressing a shudder as an older woman asked about serving it iced. Cinna watched the door closing behind Tom. The temple bells on the hanging chain shook her out of her reverie as Magdalena's customers departed. She fixed herself a pot of tea as her partner rang up the morning's receipts.

"Not bad." Magdalena came over to where she had seated herself at a corner table to take a break while the shop was empty. She leaned over and wafted the aroma arising from the white china teapot toward her, closing her eyes and breathing deeply.

"Darjeeling. Girl, you are so predictable." Magdalena opened her dark eyes and pulled out the chair across from her.

"But I always like it." She shrugged. "There's a reason they call it the Cadillac of teas."

"And here we are in the house of five hundred flavors." Magdalena lifted an arm and swept the room. "Or more and you stick with the old tried and true."

"I'm never disappointed."

"Or surprised. This is Vegas. Be a little adventurous. Experiment. How are we supposed to introduce our patrons to the wonderful world of tea if you don't lead the way? Maybe going to the awards banquet this weekend is the thing that will get you off your duff."

"Tom Marco? Spare me." *Ow*. The sip she took of her tea was too hot. She shivered, closed her eyes, and swallowed.

"Yeah, that six-foot-four-something with killer eyes and shoulders out to here is hard to take." Magdalena grinned and winked.

"You don't know him, Mags. What a waste of time loser. He was involved with my sister in college back in Des Moines 'til he dumped her, dropped out of school, and disappeared. Good riddance." She stared at her cup.

"Well, I don't know about that part." Magdalena got up to get a cinnamon bun from the day-old display.

And she'd never hear the whole story from her. Cinna took a measured sip from her cup.

"What I've heard is that he finished his degree in hotel management at UNLV while working at different places around town. Then after he and Gentleman Jim McMasters got acquainted, he worked like a dog during the Imperial's renovation. I was dancing at the Silver Strike then, dreaming about how I could open my own business and scouting around for something affordable. The downtown area north of the Strip here was just starting to pick up. The Ogden Street area is still kind of rundown, but the Imperial has helped change things. There's a reason they're up for best small independent hotel casino of the year. And if they win it..." She gave a low whistle and rubbed her thumb and forefingers together. "It can mean major, major money."

Cinna poured herself another cup, cradling it between her fingers, feeling its warmth. There no denying her sister's old flame gave her goose bumps for more reasons than one.

"Maybe he's turned over a new leaf. People do change. Cut him some slack. After all, it's been a long time since Des Moines. You were both young then. Lots of water under the bridge. How long has it been?"

"Twelve years. No, thirteen." Then four weeks ago, he had come into the shop, eyes fixed on her, as she stood caught in the act of pouring cream and honey. That face with its sun-brown hair and dark hazel eyes, the crook in his nose only adding strength to the strong plates of his face as he stared at her. It was a face more rugged than handsome. The glint of green in his eyes when he smiled had once been the thing her girlish daydreams had been made of.

Thirteen years since the last time she'd seen him at their home in Des Moines, waiting for Rose as she tripped down the stairs, her face glowing. If the slam of the door when her sister returned hadn't raised the household, her muffled sobs that night had.

"Look how we changed, Cinna. Who would have predicted a fine arts major and chemistry student would end up brewing tea in Las Vegas?"

After sporadic correspondence following graduation, Magdalena had contacted her just as the small start-up pharmaceutical company she'd worked for began another round of layoffs. Magdalena, carb-starved and tired of the weekly weigh-ins to keep her job in the chorus line of the Silver Strike Casino, had explained her dream of opening a tea bar in Las Vegas. She could remember it like it was yesterday.

"You wouldn't believe it, Cinna. I've done a survey. There isn't a single tea bar in Vegas."

"And doesn't that tell you something?"

But her former roommate's relentless enthusiasm

had carried her along. Five-nine with shoulder-length, curly brown hair sweeping her shoulders and dark eyes under feathered lashes, she had wondered more than once if Magdalena Kasas had some gypsy blood in her background. Anyway with her own carefully planned career track petering out, the possibility of any job was more tempting than unemployment, and so last year, she'd changed her address.

"SpecialTeas," she muttered.

"What?" Magdalena was working a raisin out of her bun.

"He misread it. You remember. He came in thinking this was a T-shirt place."

"Oh, Tom. Right. That was pretty funny. I wonder if he ever did find a place to print shirts for their tournament."

One month ago…

She rested her head on a hand, looking around at the teashop with its cream-colored walls and framed antique maps of the tea world—India, Ceylon, China. Plantation shutters shut out the glare of the desert sun and the street noise of America's fastest growing city. They'd created a place to have a soothing cup of tea or something light to eat. A place to read a newspaper, use a laptop, collect oneself. A quiet oasis apart from the neon overload of Las Vegas until…

A month ago Tom had entered the shop, striding up to the counter where she'd been filling her customer's cup of Devonshire Delight with a stream of cream and honey letting the cup overflow as she froze in astonishment, powerless to move or even breathe.

"Cinnamon Smith? Cinnamon," he'd said.

Since then nothing had been the same.

Of all the teashops in the entire world, why had he had to walk into theirs? Sleepless nights had followed twelve-hour days on her feet.

"Well, girlfriend, I figure there's a reason he's been a regular this last month." Magdalena interrupted her thoughts. "And any man who tips the way he does is welcome here. Don't tell me he's doing it because he's a tea lover. I know it's wicked of me, but I can't help watching as he manfully makes his way through every new blend you spring on him."

"I can't say I have much sympathy for him."

"Hey, more customers like him and we may move into the plus column. Especially if we can score a standing order from the Imperial. And if they take down one of the awards Saturday night...Wow! Purveyors of fine tea to one of North Vegas's up and coming hotels? Sounds good to me. Speaking of which I'm going to work on those gift samples Tom requested." She pushed her chair away from the table. "And if T.M. isn't coming in because he has a taste for tea, you know what he is here for."

"Spare me. He passed once on the Smith women. I hardly think he's interested now. And look where we are, Mags. The showgirl capital of the world."

Magdalena raised an eyebrow.

"Hmm. Interesting isn't it...that he couldn't come up with another date?"

"He barely notices me. You're the one he talks to. I walk by and he looks the other way."

"Like he's afraid something might show? That he'd give something away? How many men in their thirties sweat being around an attractive female like that?"

"I'm the kid sister of his old girlfriend. He used to

give me lifts to band practice."

"Yeah, well. I still say we can work the hometown angle." Beside the cash register, the telephone jangled. Magdalena picked up her napkin and dismembered bun, dumping them in the trash. She cradled the phone between her head and shoulder as she dusted her fingers.

"Hello. SpecialTeas, Las Vegas's premier tea emporium." She stopped to listen. "Yes, of course." She curled a finger at Cinna and held out the receiver. "For you."

"Who is it?"

Her partner shrugged as she handed over the phone.

"Hello?"

"Cinnamon, guess who?"

Speak of the devil. The "It" girl.

****

"So how's it look?" Magdalena looked up as she pushed open the door to their workroom. Her partner punched a hole in one of their business cards, threaded the ribbon through it, and made a bow. "I'm going with blue and red ribbons. They match the colors in the British flag. Continue with the Imperial's U.K. theme, you know. What do you think?"

"Looks good." Cinna took the muslin bundle Magdalena was holding out and balanced it on her hand. "So what are you putting in them?"

"Eight tea bags. I thought about putting a scone, but since we don't use preservatives I wasn't sure how well they'd keep. I put in two bags of our British blend, a Darjeeling, and an oolong, along with a green tea and a white one and a couple of our new Celestial Harmony mix."

Cinna ruffled the ribbon with a finger. "Maybe we could add a coupon for a breakfast bun or a scone if they visit the shop."

Magdalena stopped what she was doing to look at her, her eyes widening. "What an idea! Promote our foot traffic and give them a chance to shop."

Cinna moved over to the worktable, picking up a roll of ribbon, and pulling out a length. She studied it and found a pair of pinking shears.

"You look a million miles away." Magdalena held out a hand as she cut the ribbon. "Bad news?"

"No, just complicated. The call was from Rosemary."

"Oh, your sister."

"Yeah, the *It* girl."

"Cinna!"

"Well, you know her. Do you disagree? Tall, blonde, stacked. Skin to die for. Rose got the beauty, Sage got the brains, and me…" She shrugged. "The leftovers."

"Who was it that graduated with honors and a place on the homecoming court?"

"Come on. Prairie State was so small we practically took turns for things. Next to Rose, I'm the *Ish* girl. Blond*ish* hair, blu*ish* eyes, short*ish*. Now you can add thirty*ish* too."

"Don't put yourself down. You'd have plenty of male attention if you weren't stuck here with me working 24/7 in our tea convent. What could we call it? St. Cinnamon's House of Perpetual Steam?" She giggled as Cinna rolled her eyes.

"That sounds like something on one of those

nauseating fliers they try to hand out down on the Strip."

"Well, it's not like SpecialTeas attracts a big male clientele here. So, what's happening with Miss American Beauty Rose back in Chicago?"

Cinna cut another length of ribbon and made a face at her partner.

"That's the complication. She's not in Chicago. She's on her way here."

"Here? To Vegas?"

"Yeah, funny isn't it how the universe works? There's some kind of medical get together or seminar out here she wants to go to. I was so stunned I pretty much blanked out. I mean I've been here for almost a year now and this is the time she decides to come visit."

"Wow, and you're dating her old hometown heartthrob."

"Mags, we're not dating! This is strictly a one-time deal, believe me. I'm just going to that dinner with Tom because he wants, well, not arm candy, but maybe…arm company."

"Sure." Magdalena drew out the word as she nodded.

"Actually I'm rethinking the whole thing." She twisted the ribbon around a finger, avoiding looking at her partner. "Rose and Tom didn't part on good turns. If she's going to be around this weekend maybe I should…" She lifted a shoulder.

"Cancel out? Cinna! You don't want to do that." Magdalena looked aghast.

"I know, I know, I know. Think about the business."

"I don't want to sound crass, but this could be our

break here, girl. Tom Marco is Jim McMasters' main man. And Gentleman Jim is the chairman of the board of the Imperial, an 800 room upscale property just full of potential tea drinkers. And being a Brit, he probably has Earl Grey running in his veins. Getting a standing order from the Imperial? This could make or break us."

"I know." She closed her eyes and massaged the back of her head. Things had gotten a lot more complicated since she'd opened up that morning.

"I'm not asking you to do anything other than just be friendly with Tom. Smile, be pleasant, and let our products speak for themselves."

She nodded.

"I know you've got doubts about him, but people do change. It's just the one night. Go to the awards dinner on Saturday and talk up SpecialTeas to everyone. Meanwhile, we'll be giving the Imperial a chance to sample our product line with these little babies." Magdalena waved a bundle in her direction.

"Right. Right."

"Honestly, this could be our foot in the door. Even downtown where we are, Las Vegas real estate is pricy. We're making up the shortfall in proceeds every month out of our dwindling savings. You know what getting this business going has entailed."

Cinna opened her eyes and picked up the scissors again. "Rose did say they'd be staying somewhere on the Strip. Maybe I can keep the two of them apart so she doesn't have to run into Tom again."

"They'd? So she's not coming alone?"

"No, there's some other medical-type person with her, I think. I really didn't pay much attention. I don't know if he's another dentist or what."

"Maybe a nail technician?" Magdalena giggled. "What's the name of your sister's business?"

"It's Masterpiece Manor now. They decided against Tooth and Nail once they had other beauty aestheticians involved. Now they have massage therapists, hairdressers, and a dermatologist along with a relaxation guru and a plastic surgeon. Rosemary's practice is cosmetic dentistry. Whitening, porcelain veneers, invisible braces." The harmonious blend of facial form and function, her sister's advertising proclaimed.

"Your family has always had a wicked sense of humor."

Yeah, it was something Fred and Ginger Smith had been known for, but right now their middle child wasn't laughing.

Chapter Two

Cinna balanced her canvas tote bags and shook her head at a flower vendor offering the usual plastic wrapped bouquets for sale. She wove her way through the crowd already gathering to watch the Fremont Street Experience. The light and laser show featuring streams of jet fighters, galloping buffalo, a space odyssey, and, because it was Vegas, dancing girls, was projected several times nightly onto the ninety-foot latticework steel mesh canopy that arched over the pedestrian part of Fremont Street. Hopefully, some of the assembled crowd would find their way to the Fremont Street Extension mini-mall afterward and refresh themselves with a cup of fresh-brewed tea.

"Excuse-moi, m'lle." A juggler on a unicycle circled around her.

The Imperial Hotel-Casino stood on Ogden Street, a block north of Fremont. It hadn't been worth the bother of getting her car out. The area was historic for being the site where the east and west rail lines had connected, along with having the city's first traffic signal, telephone, and paved street, as well as boasting its first casino.

On Ogden the crowds thinned. She shifted her bags and crossed the street. Magdalena had Googled James McMasters and the Imperial Hotel for her shortly after Tom had mistakenly entered SpecialTeas. It had been hard not to be impressed. The Imperial's principal investor, McMasters was a former RAF officer, still ramrod straight at eighty plus. During his former career as an engineer, he had developed patents on energy-saving equipment for cars. A widower seeking a sunnier climate than his native Britain, he'd arrived in Vegas several years before.

Magdalena said rumor had it that one night he'd fallen into conversation with an assistant barkeep and then taken him to see a north Vegas property he had looked at earlier that day as an investment possibility. The following week McMasters had returned to England, lined up investors, bought out the management of the failing Outpost Hotel Casino, and back in Vegas, hired Tom, his bar acquaintance, to help him with reinventing the property.

The renovated Imperial Hotel Casino dominated its block. A limousine was pulled up under the porte-cochere while an old-style London taxi stood under the green and white awning at the side of the building, probably ready to provide shuttle service for guests. Magdalena had said a number of investors had urged the implosion of the original property and then rebuilding on the site, but McMasters and Tom had opted to scour and polish the original nineteenth century structure as well as adding on. Windows and façade sparkling now in the bright sun, it looked like they had made the right choice.

"Ma'am." A doorman in top hat and white gloves got the door for her.

She caught her breath as she entered. Should she have changed her clothing before coming over? Upscale? Oh, yes. And she was still wearing her "Have a cuppa" T-shirt and wrap-around skirt from the shop. She lifted her chin and crossed the marble parquet floor to where several people stood behind a desk.

Wouldn't dressing up for the occasion have sent the wrong signal to Tom?

As if he cared.

At the check-in counter, a woman wearing a blue blazer looked up from her computer screen. Full-figured with shoulder-length, graying black hair, her nametag read Dolores Rivera Ruiz, Assistant Manager.

"Hello, how may I help you?" she asked giving her a warm smile.

"Hi, my name is Cinnamon Smith. My partner and I own the SpecialTeas shop in the Fremont Street Extension Mall. I have a delivery here for Tom Marco. He had asked us to bring him some samples of our products for you to try."

"Oh, great. Aren't you prompt?" The woman's smile broadened. "Tom just told me about it earlier. I think I've seen your store. Isn't it close to the jeweler's over there?"

"Right, Jailhouse Rock Jewelry. They're just next door to us."

"I've been in there. I bought a turquoise-inlaid bolo for my husband's birthday. They have so many unique one-of-kind things. I guess they make a lot of it themselves."

"Yes, Adam was a geology student at UNLV and his wife has a degree in fine arts. They prospect for garnet up around Ely."

"Well, I'll stop by for a cup of tea the next time I'm over that way. Mr. Marco is away right now on errands, but let me see if I can track down Gentleman

Jim for you."

So she wouldn't be seeing Tom again. *That was good, wasn't it?*

Cinna boosted her sacks up onto the desk and watched the lobby as Mrs. Ruiz picked up a house phone and hit some numbers with practiced taps of her manicured fingers. After the walk through the crowded streets, the air conditioning was a relief. The lobby was a show in itself. Below the crystal chandelier, a fountain was spraying water. As it fell, it cascaded down through a series of rocks where multi-colored fish wove changing patterns between lily pads.

"Miss Smith?"

She turned back to the desk.

"Gentleman Jim has just concluded his daily whist game in our Exeter Club and would like to meet you for an aperitif in Draughts. It's our informal bar. If you'll come with me, I'll show you the way. Eric, can you carry Miss Smith's bags for her, please?"

"Of course." A young man tending to one of the lobby's overflowing pots of tropical blooms put down his clippers and moved to collect her things.

"I don't want to impose. I could just leave all this here for him."

"Please, it's no bother. Mr. McMasters would love to meet a friend of Tom's."

"Well, we're not really..." The words were on her lips before she choked them off. *Remember, this could be our chance at the big time*. Magdalena had reiterated the sentiment several times before she had left. *Be friendly*. No one else needed to know what the relationship, or lack of one, was between her and Tom.

She followed Mrs. Ruiz as she made her way

around the staircase and past a cashier's cage that looked like an antique, brass bank teller's cage. It had been conveniently positioned across from the action of the casino area. She stopped for a moment with Eric while the assistant manager had a word with a housekeeper in an old-fashioned, ruffled maid's cap.

A low murmur of British invasion music came from the entrance to the bar. Draughts had apparently been designed to resemble a British pub with mahogany and cherry fixtures and massive beams. Above the beveled glass behind the bar, a television was quietly showing an English football match. From a corner table, an older white-haired gentleman raised a hand to wave as Dolores wove her way between the tables.

Cinna gave him her hand as he stood and Dolores introduced them.

"So delighted to meet you, my dear. Cinnamon, what a perfectly delicious name!" He covered her hand with his other.

"I guess my parents thought so." It hadn't been the easiest of names when growing up in Des Moines.

"So is there a whole spice set? Spice girls and boys?"

"Just three of us—Rosemary, Cinnamon, and Sage." Fortunately, her parents' third child had been a boy since Nutmeg had been a possibility for another daughter.

"Capital, capital. And your T-shirt…how droll! Don't you think so, Dolores? Have a cuppa. Marvelous."

"Yes, it's wonderful. Eric, why don't you put Miss Smith's things down over there?"

"Oh, yes, do. Thank you both for escorting

Cinnamon here. You don't mind if I call you that, do you? You Americans are so casual." Tom's boss moved to hold a chair for her.

"Please do."

"Just a topping name," James McMasters said reseating himself. "Of course, around Vegas I'm known as Gentleman Jim which I do admit I rather like. Now you must tell me all about your business. Young Thomas has been most keen on your enterprise."

"Well…" Were her cheeks reddening? She drew a breath as her courtly white-haired host leaned forward, clasping his hands and smiling encouragingly at her.

"We've been open now for eight months. I came out about a year ago. My friend Magdalena was already living and working here. The business was her brainchild. Our shop is in the Fremont Street Extension mini-mall. We have a few tables in the front, but most of our business is carryout. We develop and serve organic teas along with a variety of items such as scones, muffins, and buns. We're pretty small. It's still just the two of us."

She could feel her heart racing. Was she babbling? She wasn't coming on too strong, was she?

"Wonderful. I have high hopes of persuading Thomas away from that sludge he calls his morning coffee into a taste for the civilized life."

"I don't know about that, sir. He's been a good customer, but I don't think we've converted him."

"Oh, Jim, please. Her Majesty hasn't knighted me yet. Obviously, he's found something to his liking at your establishment." McMasters reached over to pat her hand.

She bit her lip. Was the strain of dealing with her

host's well-meant pleasantries showing?

A waiter appeared in period Edwardian costume in response to McMasters's raised hand. Black armbands encircled pushed up puffy sleeves.

"What would you have, my dear? Pasqual can bring you a fruit juice or lemonade, if you please. Perhaps a nice gin shanty? We also carry our own micro-brewed draft beer and the usual pub grub—fish and chips, bangers and mash. Are you hungry?"

"Lemonade will be fine, thank you."

"With ice, yes? You Americans do like things chilled, don't you? Another one of these please." McMasters lifted his glass. "With a hair of the dog as you Yanks put it. I feel somewhat American myself. My late wife's sister married an American airman when he was over on our side during the war. Harriet and I were at their home outside Atlanta many times. Lovely area, but a bit humid for me. When I was knocking about, looking for a bit of sun, I came out west. Dryer, you know. So, Cinnamon, Thomas tells me you first met back in your hometown."

"More or less. He…" It wasn't his hometown. He'd just appeared one day, moving in with a relative, she thought, and stayed long enough to date and dump Rosemary. "He went to school for a while in Des Moines."

"Yes, the great Midwest. Tom has quite a background. Quite a varied background and not always, perhaps, the happiest. But, hopefully, all that is in the past now. We do so appreciate his work here. Thank you, Pasqual." He swapped glasses with the barman and held up his as she took her own.

"Cheers, my dear."

21

"Cheers." She took a sip. The tartness was refreshing.

"So how did you come to move out here and start a business with your friend?"

"Magdalena was my college roommate back in Iowa. After graduation, I worked for a small pharmaceutical company in Cincinnati and she came out here to try and get into show business. She was dancing in the chorus line at the Silver Strike." One of the girls keeping her clothes, such as they were, on.

"I'm acquainted with the Silver Strike. Thomas and I took in most of the hotels in town after I made the decision to stay. Seeing what the competition was and how we could better it."

"She was tired of doing three shows a night. She called me back in Cincinnati, where my job was being cut, with an idea for opening a business offering teas and pastries. She thought it would be the first of its kind here."

"I see. Yes, indeed, quite unique. So you weren't a dancer?" McMasters asked.

At five-two? Not even on tiptoe.

"No, not me. My degree is in chemistry and I was working in research and development in the medical field. Now I do some of the research on our blends, their properties, chemical compositions, that kind of thing. Magdalena has the educated palate to really put things together."

"Thomas tells me you've come up with some exotic concoctions. I look forward to sampling them." McMasters smiled genially at her.

"He's tried a few." It had become a kind of perverse pleasure watching his face as he sampled some of Magdalena's more adventurous combinations.

"So tell me what you've brought for us today."

"We've put eight of our varieties in each sample bundle along with a coupon good for a visit to the shop." She pulled out one of the muslin bundles from her bag, untied it, and took out the different teas.

Her stomach growled as a waiter carrying a loaded tray passed their table. It had been a long time since she and Magdalena had grabbed a quick lunch. She pressed a hand against her midsection. Hopefully, the Imperial's chairman wouldn't notice anything.

"Lovely presentation." McMasters reached out to touch the bow.

"Thank you. Magdalena's the artistic one. We made up fifty of them. Tom said you wanted to try them in some of your suites and on your breakfast buffet. We included some of our best-selling blends and a new one we're debuting this week called Celestial Harmony."

"Thomas is game for new things. I don't suppose he'd be in Vegas if he weren't, would you? He's an ex-Army ranger, you know. We both have that military background in common. Told me a bit about his service in Afghanistan when we met. Rough piece of business there. Managed to get his platoon out of a sticky situation, but at some cost to himself. He likes to do the outdoor thing. Rock climbing, hiking, and the like. He did an Iron Man competition once before things got so busy here at the hotel. Still wants to field a team to represent the Imperial in some kind of charity competition he hopes to set up to benefit the returning troops."

Army ranger? Charity sponsor? Maybe Tom had turned over a new leaf as Magdalena had suggested. Or sent one fluttering. Was it possible?

She was aware of Gentleman Jim's eyes watching her curiously as she frowned.

****

He tucked his mail under his free arm, balanced the tux on its hanger, got the key into the lock, and nudged the door open. He tossed the mail on the kitchenette counter and hung the tux in the closet, taking a moment to smooth down its folds under the plastic. It wasn't the latest style, but its classic appearance had appealed to him. Hopefully, it would to Cinnamon too.

"You gotta use what you got, man." He smiled to himself in encouragement.

It looked like the building's cleaning crew had been in. Not that there was ever much to do. The three-room unit was enough. He'd stayed at the Imperial for the last two years, moving from one room to another as renovations progressed. After last year's grand opening, he'd found the apartment, a place away from work where he could decompress. His needs were simple. A shower and a bed were plenty. A room at the Imperial was still designated as his, functioning now as a place to keep a change of clothes and stow some personal items more than anything else.

The kitchenette served as a place to stock refreshments and snacks. He opened the refrigerator and found the local root beer that had become his favorite since moving to Nevada. Using the magnetic church key on the door, he popped the top. He assumed the stove and oven worked although he'd never tested them. He knew the microwave could heat coffee, but that had been before he'd managed to track down Cinnamon Smith.

Small world didn't half describe how the last month had rocked his world. He took a seat on the couch, propped his legs up on the laminate coffee table, and ignored the blinking button on his answering machine. The furniture the apartment had come with had been fine. The television carried all the sports channels necessary for meaningful existence. He'd gotten by in army quarters most of his adult life. Hell, the room at the auto dealership back in Iowa had been better than some of the foster homes he'd been in, let alone life with Mom.

He found his smart phone with his free hand and checked it. *Meeting with the hotel's auditors at their office in Henderson.* That was over. He was clear until a get-together with the food service staff. Sometime he'd have to find time to brief Gentleman Jim about the auditors' findings. He took another swallow. It hadn't gone as well as he'd hoped. Maybe finding Cinnamon again had lent a rosier hue to everything in his world than was really warranted.

Oh, Jim would be philosophical. He could hear the old man's voice now. "Look, my lad, we've just passed our first anniversary. Can't expect to coin money right away. I mean look at Rome, right? Wasn't built in a day. Let's keep our chins up, you know, and soldier on."

But, he'd expected better. Letting Jim McMasters down was almost worse than hearing the disappointing news itself. How could everything seem to be going so well and they still come up short for the quarter?

Think positive.

After all, what were the odds of finding Cinnamon Smith again right under his nose? Even in Vegas where the longest of bets found takers? Leaving the Imperial last year on some long forgotten errand, he'd been crossing Fremont Street when ahead in the crowd a small figure caught his eye and he'd stopped frozen in mid-stride.

There was something about the back of that head, the straight line of the shoulders, the tangle of dark blonde curls. Had his heart stopped as well? Whatever. He'd waited too long. Before he got in gear again, whoever it was had disappeared into the milling crowd around the Golden Nugget.

Forget it. He'd been mistaken. It wasn't her. Not a chance in the world he told himself. But if it had been, if she'd been one of the million tourists Las Vegas drew yearly... Unable to sleep that night, he'd pulled out the phone book and used his staff position at the Imperial to call other hotels and ask if they had a Cinnamon Smith registered.

They didn't.

It hadn't been her.

Or if it was, she was under a different name. Maybe her husband's. He refused to do another pointless Internet search.

Over the years, Cinnamon Smith's name hadn't popped up in an on-line search. Ditto for Sage. Her parents were no longer listed in the Des Moines phone books. The national listings for Fred Smiths ran into five figures and Rosemarys for four. And he wasn't sure what kind of reception he'd get from Cinna's older sister.

At least pretend you've got some brains, he'd told himself. And he'd forgotten about it for the most part until a glimpse of two girls across the street running for the monorail station on Paradise Road stopped him again.

Above the noise of the traffic, he'd caught part of what the taller, dark-haired girl was yelling at her friend. "Hurry, Cinna, we…"

The monorail had pulled away by the time he crossed the street.

Two possible sightings? Could she be living or working in Vegas? The private detective agency the hotel used had come up dry. No Cinnamon Smith in the city directory, no listing by the Nevada Gaming Commission as working in any of the city's licensed hotels, restaurants, bars or casinos, no Nevada driver's license.

But the fact remained; he'd seen her once in the Fremont Street area and then again on a monorail heading north. It wasn't much, but for months, it had kept him scouting the downtown area on his free time. Up one street, down another. At the least, he was getting fresh air and exercise, he'd grimly reassured himself. Until four weeks ago, when she'd walked toward him on the other side of the street. He'd dodged traffic and shouted comments as he jostled his way through irate street vendors to follow her. She'd turned off the sidewalk and slipped through a wrought-iron archway into something labeled the Fremont Street Extension, an open-air mini-mall with shops on three sides. He must have passed the place hundreds of times without noticing.

On the far side of the plaza beyond the benches and potted palms, she was holding a store door open for a departing customer. He'd stopped dead in his tracks.

It was Cinna. The same Cinnamon Smith he'd met

years before when he'd taken her older sister home from class one day.

He'd been paired with Rosemary on some forgotten project in a business class. Life had landed him in Des Moines after the state had emancipated him from foster care at the age of eighteen. Odd jobs and overtime at a car dealership had provided enough to finance classes at the local community college.

Knockout didn't half describe Rosemary Smith—blonde, blue eyed, with legs that went on forever; she was the sort of girl who wouldn't have given a guy like him the time of day if he hadn't been driving one of the flashier loaners from the dealership.

But she'd let him give her a ride home to the kind of suburban, two-story real families lived in. And there had been her kid sister. He knew somehow Fred and Ginger had been present along with Rosemary's little brother, Sage. But Cinnamon…

He closed his eyes, feeling the condensation from the bottle like the sweat on his hands when she'd looked up at him from the picnic table where she'd been setting things out in their backyard.

Cinnamon—huge blue-gray eyes, curling lashes under her arched brows, a stray blonde curl catching the edge of her wide mouth, its lower lip pouting provocatively. Sweet and hot as her name. He'd wanted that mouth under his

He blew out a breath, remembering. Thirteen years later, he could still see her standing there like it was yesterday—tanned legs under her cut-offs, white gym shoes, Band Rat T-shirt. God, he was taken.

Somehow he and Rose had become a couple. He'd tried to talk himself into accepting his good fortune, to breathe normally when Cinna slid out of his car after he and Rose had given her a lift somewhere, strutting off, her little ass swaying in accompaniment to the bounce of her ponytail as his hands gripped the steering wheel. A twenty-one year old man with more of the rough side of life under his belt than most adults, falling for a seventeen year old kid.

Tried to pretend until that climatic night when things blew up with Rosemary. Hopefully, she had moved on to better things.

In disbelief, he had followed Cinna into the shop and up to the counter where she was waiting on a customer. Teashop? It could have been a bowling alley for all he'd noticed. He'd been focused on one thing. Cinna had looked up at him as she had more than a dozen years and a thousand miles ago and he'd been just as tongue-tied as ever.

Oh, it was more than clear her feelings weren't the same as his. Yet.

Campaigns may not be won on the first day, but they can sure be lost as they'd taught them at Officers' Candidate School. Remember—preparation, patience, and follow-through.

He tipped back his bottle and drained it.

He'd made up some lame excuse he didn't remember. Her business partner, the tall brunette he'd seen her with on the Strip, had come over and Cinna had introduced him.

"Tom Marco from Des Moines." She hadn't sounded thrilled.

"From Vegas now." He'd extended his hand. "I'm over at the Imperial, the old Outpost Casino, you know."

"That Tom Marco, sure!"

Magdalena had laughed, shaken hands with him, and explained about their shop while Cinna had stood silent. Since then he'd been a regular, not missing one of the six and a half days a week they were open, steeling himself to drink his way through a never-ending array of their offerings.

It helped to have someone else around. There was no denying Cinna's friend seemed happier to see him than she did. He had the feeling she was on his side. Magdalena chatted about the shop, asking about the Imperial, his opinion on local suppliers, pulling Cinna into the conversation. Cinna seemed to avoid their mutual past as if it was planted with land mines, but gradually, information had emerged. Fred and Ginger had retired to Florida where Fred was selling maritime insurance now. Sage was in graduate school on the East coast and Rose lived in the Chicago area. If Cinna hadn't appeared enthusiastic about his reappearance in her life, at least she seemed to have relaxed a bit. She wasn't hunching her shoulders and retreating a step when he entered the shop now. And there was no ring on her finger, no gentleman callers he had tripped over while drinking tea.

He put his head back on the couch and stretched out.

She'd accepted his date for the awards banquet. He'd worked at phrasing it casually. Kept it low-key. Evidently, it had done the trick. Just going out to a dinner, no big deal, not a real date.

Oh, but it was.

He folded his hands across his middle and willed himself to relax. Strategic campaigns aren't won in a day.

Thirteen years ago, he'd wanted her.

He still did.

This was a campaign he meant to win.

Chapter Three

Tom checked his watch as he stepped on the elevator. Terrance and Roxane should just be finishing their shift on surveillance and he wanted to touch base on how their day had gone before they clocked out. The meeting with Food and Beverage Services had run long, but afterward, he'd been able to set up his private agenda for the evening. He'd squeezed in time then to see Jim McMasters and bring him up to speed on what the auditors had found. As he'd expected, the older man had been philosophical.

"Coming close, aren't we, Thomas?" he'd said with a shrug. "Can see that corner we'll be turning right up ahead."

But it had been a year and with so many of the ideas for renovation and remodeling his, it felt like the responsibility for showing a profit should fall on his shoulders. The elevator stopped on the mezzanine and Dolores Ruiz stepped in and raised a hand in greeting.

"Hey, boss man, what's happening? Haven't seen you since early this morning."

"Pretty good. The meeting with Food and Beverage ran over."

"Yeah, foodies are always way more interested in that stuff than the rest of us. They could talk about it for hours if you'd let them."

"I'm on my way up to see our eye in the sky crew

before they leave. How's your day been? You going to be able to get out of here on time?"

"Should. I just need to check on housekeeping on nine. Someone reported a problem with a slow shower. The gal from the tea shop was here with the samples you ordered."

"That was quick. I was just in there the other day."

"I took her to meet Gentleman Jim. He still enjoys a pretty face. Later, I had housekeeping put the gift packages in the suites reserved for the tournament. I'll put the rest out on the breakfast buffet tomorrow."

"Sounds good." He cleared his throat. "I'm going to be taking her, Cinnamon, I mean, to the awards banquet." He waited as the elevator stopped and the doors opened to admit more people.

"I've known her for a while. She comes from my hometown." *At least one of them.* A variety of foster homes made for a long list. "How about you? Are you up for Saturday?"

"Got my dress and dancing shoes. Brielle is going to be my date."

"Leon not interested?" he asked.

Dolores shook her head.

"You couldn't get that man in black tie and tux with a high caliber weapon. Especially not when there's a playoff game that night."

He nodded. "Yeah, we're getting a lot action down in the sports book."

The British Open, their sports betting room, was one of the Imperial's most consistently profitable areas.

"Girls home yet?"

"No, their semester isn't over 'til the end of this month." Dolores rolled her eyes. "There's something to be said for having your kids close together, but putting them through college isn't one of them."

"I'll remember that."

"Anyway, Brielle's earned her ticket to the banquet. She's done a bang-up job with day shift supervision since she started."

"Since a lot always seems to be needed."

Dolores made a face and shrugged as the elevator stopped on her floor and she stepped off.

Terrance and Roxane both had their chairs pushed back and were briefing the night shift as he entered the darkened room. Surveillance cameras under smoky glass domes swept every public area of the hotel property sending the feed to the monitors in the office and saving the action on disc for possible later review. Terrance turned his way and waved him over. Both security officers were veterans at spotting trouble before it got out of control.

"Hi. What's going on?"

"Just bringing Jacki and Malina up to speed. Let me rewind something." The tech played with his computer monitor and the footage from the casino floor froze then jerked backward.

"Okay, here we are about eleven-fifteen this morning. Marcia Burton, the blackjack dealer, buzzed us so we honed in on the table. She said later she was worried about a possible card counter, but the gentleman was gone by the time Brielle picked up our page and got over to watch."

"Brielle?"

It wouldn't have been her job.

"Yeah, well, she came over with the pit boss. She stood and observed play for a while anyway and picked up on something else. This gal…" Terrance tapped the screen with his finger where an older woman in a pants suit was sitting at the end of the table, "was low stacking when she pushed in bets."

The term referred to replacing a higher value chip with a lower value one at the bottom of the stack.

"Marcia didn't catch it?"

"No, it gets more interesting. Watch the blonde at the end."

He leaned forward to study an animated young woman at the other end of the table talking to the dealer. Somewhere in her twenties, she was laughing and giggling.

"She was asking Marcia questions?"

"Right, acting like she wasn't familiar with the game. Could be trying to distract Marcia's attention from what the older gal was up to, working as a tag team."

He nodded. Dealers always tried to help novices as much as they could. It encouraged them to stay and play.

"Brielle notified floor security. Here come Luis and Scott T."

He watched the two uniformed guards flank the older woman and spread her chips out on the green felt as she looked up to gape at them. In a manner of seconds, they had taken her arms and were quietly leading her away.

"What's the story?"

"The usual. She's new in town, was confused by the different chips, made an honest mistake, has never been in trouble. You've heard it all before. Same sad story. They took her to the Security office and called the LVPD. If she doesn't know any attempt to cheat a casino is a felony in Nevada, she's about to learn."

"And Blondie?"

"Gone with the wind." At five-foot nothing and similar girth, no one had argued with Roxane Cox when she formerly had worked security at the Outpost and they didn't in her new position at the Imperial either.

"Neither of them is listed in the black book." Roxane referred to the list of known cheats banned from all casino property in the city. "We'll get a picture printed up of Miss Tank Top and keep an eye out for her."

"Sounds good." He straightened up. "Any other excitement?"

"Nah." Terrance got up from his monitor. "We watched a few wanderers waiting for them to try a chip dip into someone's basket or open bag, but everyone stayed honest today."

"So where was Ron, our day shift supervisor when Marcia ran into trouble at her table?" He walked away from the bank of monitors as Malina Ramos slid into the seat Terrance had vacated.

It was automatic to watch her legs. Every male with a pulse did. The tall Philippine beauty had been a headliner at one of the properties on the Strip until a wrong turn in heels ended in a broken ankle and wrenched kneecap. When the Imperial was getting set for its re-opening, she'd come to the hiring fair asking for a desk job.

He raised an eyebrow in inquiry looking over at his day surveillance crew.

Roxane glanced away while Terrance put his hands on his hips and shook his head.

"Missing in action."

"That Innie versus Outie thing still gets to some people, chief," Roxane said.

The Outies were former Outpost employees like Roxane, Ron, and the Imperial's Chief of Security, Don Davis, who had come back to work at the Imperial while the Innies were fresh hires. Most employees of the old Outpost had accepted the fact the Imperial was doing things differently. For others like Ron, the change still grated.

"I'm not excusing Ron, but since he managed the old Outpost. He thinks he ought to have your job, or at least Dolores's. It bugs him big time that she went from being head of housekeeping at the Cosmopolitan to becoming assistant manager here," Roxane said. "She'd worked her way up over there from waitressing to manning the desk on night shift to a staff position."

"Yeah, and like Ron was such a success," Terrance snorted. "If he hadn't poured free shots for everyone he knew in Vegas, maybe the Outpost wouldn't have gone under."

"Yeah, well, he's had a lot on his plate on the home front too, you know. Losing his son in the motorcycle accident, then his wife climbing back in the bottle."

Ron again. The matter had come to an ugly head at last month's general staff meeting. He could have handled it better. Ron had felt singled out for criticism. Since then, he'd tried to cut him some slack out of guilt over what he was dealing with in his personal life, but apparently, that wasn't working either. Jim McMasters didn't like firing anyone, but it looked like it would come to that, especially with Ron's assistant Brielle stepping up to the plate like she was, doing his job as well as her own.

Roxane was studying him. Their eyes met.

"Well, you gotta do what you gotta do, chief."

"So is he back now?"

"Yeah." Terrance pointed to the monitor Jacki Fisher was watching. "We picked him up a little while ago in the baccarat room chatting up players."

"Great." There was a sour taste in his mouth. Baccarat drew many of their high rollers, sophisticated gamblers not generally amused by recycled stories about the glory days of the old Vegas. Ron definitely wasn't the face the Imperial was trying to present to the public now.

"Well, I'll let you go. Enjoy your evening." Terrance raised a hand and Roxane gave him a mock salute as he left.

He checked his watch again. It was going to be tight but he thought he could do it. He skipped the elevator for the stairs.

****

He took a second to compose himself, squared his shoulders, and opened the door. Behind him, the evening noise of the pedestrian mall faded. Cinna looked up from where she was clearing off a table. Magdalena waved at him as she came out of the back.

"We're getting ready to close. I'm sorry, Tom, but I just emptied the tea machine," Magdalena apologized.

He breathed a sigh of relief.

"I can fix you up a quick pot though. It won't take long," she offered.

"No, never mind, I'm fine." He held up his hands in protest.

Cinna hoisted her tray of dirty dishes up onto the

counter. His stomach tightened. He bit his lip and resisted the impulse to play the gentleman and help her with it. Stay cool, he reminded himself. It wouldn't help things to crowd her.

"I was over at the Imperial today." Cinna separated the silverware, placing it in a dish drainer. "It's wonderful, first time I'd been inside. Your assistant Dolores took me to meet Mr. McMasters. I didn't want to bother him, but she insisted he'd like to meet me."

"He's a charmer, isn't he?" Magdalena said. "I heard him speak once at a Downtown Business Owners' Association meeting. He had us eating out of his hand. I understand he's a real war hero, too. That he actually flew in the Battle of Britain."

"He lied about his age to get in," Tom said. "I guess during the last years of the war, they weren't real careful about checking birth certificates. Thank you for stopping in. We've distributed the samples you left."

"Thanks for giving us a try." Looking up from what she was doing, Cinna smiled. A real one, not the kind she sometimes provided when her friend prodded her. He'd been in the shop often enough to know the difference.

Point for the home team.

"Yes, we appreciate it." Magdalena arched her back and stretched.

"Happy to do it. Actually, I came by to ask you ladies to dinner."

Cinna stopped in the act of picking up her tray again to look at him.

"One of our dining venues is premiering a new menu tonight. They presented the dishes at our Food and Beverage Services meeting this afternoon and I'd welcome the company and input."

"I don't know," Cinna said slowly. "Mags?"

"Not me, thanks. I want to hang around here and wait on the call from David. He's our tea scout," she explained. "He's in this country now. He's been working his way down the west coast from Vancouver and was in the Tahoe area Monday. I want to find out when he's going to be heading our way."

"You have a tea scout?"

"Right." Magdalena found a bottle of cleaning spray and a roll of paper towels under the counter and moved over to the table area.

"His name is David Witheroe and he's from New Zealand. We've never meet in person, have we, Cinna? A friend of mine in Seattle recommended him and we got together over the Internet. He travels all over Asia sending back things for us to try. Like the goji berries from Tibet. They promote good vision, circulation, and have tons of anti-aging benefits. You may remember that tea from a week or so ago, Tom."

"It had that pinky tinge to it," Cinna volunteered.

Oh, he remembered it.

"Anyway, he's supposed to give me a call and firm up a time to be in Vegas. He's pretty much of a free spirit as you can imagine. So I'm just going to hang around here and get a few things done we've been putting off, but you go on with Tom, Cinna," she said as she straightened up from polishing the tabletop.

"I don't know." Cinnamon took off her apron and turned toward him, her T-shirt curving nicely over her chest. "I'm not dressed to go out, Tom. I appreciate the offer, but really—"

"You look fine." *More than fine.*

"Come on, Cinna. You deserve a night out. We both do and maybe when David lands in town I can get one myself. We've been slaves to the tea trade ever since we opened. And who picked up the slack after we canceled our janitorial service last month to pinch pennies?"

"But look at me." She plucked at her top and looked down at her bare legs in their sandals. "I've seen the Imperial, Tom. I'm not dressed for it."

"It's the Cork and Cleaver, our casual dining restaurant. It's situated between the pub grub fare we offer at Draughts and our white linen establishment, the Reserve. It's just family dining."

"Go, go, go." Magdalena took the apron out of her friend's unresisting hands. "Put this man out of his misery. I'll take my time finishing up here. David will call when he does. When was the last time you had a night out?"

"Or you."

"I've got plans to change that. I'm a sucker for an accent." Magdalena picked up Cinna's tray and nudged the louvered door to the back open with a practiced swing of her hip.

"It's been a long day, I should probably just…" Cinnamon's voice faltered as he covered her hand on the counter with his, caressing her warm knuckles until he reminded himself not to.

"Should just, um…" He saw her swallow.

"Here, girl." Magdalena returned carrying a purse. "Here's your bag. Now get out of here. Have a good dinner, relax for once, and tell me about the high life tomorrow. I'm just going to putter around here and wait on David's call."

He straightened, held his breath, and waited as she circled the counter.

"Well, then, I guess…it's a go."

Magdalena gave them a smile and wave as he followed Cinna to the door.

Outside the sidewalks were crowded, the heat still palpable as people made their way to the first show of the evening at the Fremont Street Experience with its two million lights. Casino and restaurant employees were busy urging handouts and coupons on passers-by. He nodded at the store on the corner, "Lotsa Slots," as they waited for the light to change. The sign on the window read "Classic Slot Machines Available For Home Purchase—Legal in Most States!"

"We're a regular customer of this place," he said.

"Oh, Lotsa Slots. Do you use their machines?"

"No, but the owner seems to be the only one in North Vegas with the know how to service the machines in our slots room which go down regularly. When we remodeled, Jim thought it would be fun to go with the old-fashioned, one-armed bandits. And it has been a draw. There's no question that people enjoy them. It's one of our busiest areas. When the blinking lights and ringing bells signal a jackpot win, one of our slots attendants comes over to take a picture. Unfortunately, they're temperamental and break down so often we have the owner here on a regular schedule to come in for maintenance."

"Joe Niemeyer. He's a customer of ours. Every Monday, I'm there with a double Darjeeling and almond biscotti for him."

He took her elbow as the light changed and they threaded their way across.

"So do you do your own baking?" he asked.

"Not any more. Thank goodness, that's something we delegated. We found a bakery nearby to produce the recipes Magdalena and I had accumulated. The food items are pretty much a break-even category, but we figure they help bring in people making a breakfast stop. We're still pretty much treading water right now, looking for the big sale." Her voice trailed off as she glanced up at him nervously.

He pretended not to notice.

"Breaking even is a big first step. We're looking forward to it ourselves." He took her arm as they turned into the Imperial's circular drive.

Brian, the doorman, trotted back after helping an elderly couple into a cab to hold the door for them. Tom followed Cinna inside.

Automatically, he paused to survey the lobby. Chairs at all the proper angles, carpeted areas swept, plants trimmed. Light from the mezzanine windows poured through as music played discreetly in the background. From where she was standing beside the desk, Brielle Bennett gave him a bright smile.

He looked down to see Cinna watching him.

"Everything pass inspection?"

"Looks shipshape. Let's go this way." He took her hand and pointed past the desk and the bank of elevators.

"As you can see, we've stuck to a British theme throughout the property. The Reserve, up on the penthouse level, is our gourmet dining experience in the tradition of a fine English club. It's got a great view at night and the bookings have been steadily growing."

A roar of laughter came from the entrance to

Draughts as they passed.

"The pub seems popular too."

"Yeah, it's taken off. Our sports book, where wagering on football, baseball, boxing, all that kind of thing, is done is over there." He pointed to a line of bettors standing in front of a row of cashiers under a changing table of odds. Cinnamon paused in the entry to watch. The rear of the room held a tiered amphitheater where people sat or stood to watch the simulcast of a horserace in progress on a large screen. Other wide screen plasma televisions and computer terminals, leather armchairs, desks, and shelves of sporting publications were clustered around the room. He stooped down to pick up a discarded tip sheet from the floor.

"Draughts gets a lot of business from people celebrating a win or drowning a loss. And down here is our destination." He touched her fingers as she followed him. "The Cork and Cleaver is our adaptation of an English inn."

He stopped beside a podium at the entrance where the host was approaching.

The young man smiled and bowed his head. "Mr. Marco. We're glad you and your guest could join us tonight. This way please if you're ready."

He scanned the room as Cinna followed their host. Half full, it looked as if everyone was having a good time as they perused menus, enjoyed a drink, or selected offerings from the dessert cart, but at the height of the dinner hour, business could definitely be better. He thought he recognized a man dining by himself as a local food critic from one of the Las Vegas trade papers. He crossed his fingers. The table he'd selected earlier was at the edge of the room by a gas fireplace hearth under an oil painting of a rural scene. She had a view of the room while he could focus on her.

"Can I bring you both something from the bar, sir?"

"Cinna, what would you like?"

"Oh, nothing for me." She looked up at their host, her dark blonde curls tumbling about her throat. There was a spot on her neck where he could see her pulse throbbing. If he leaned over he could kiss the warm, soft flesh there.

"Mr. Marco?"

"Come on, Cinna," he urged. "Celebrate a bit."

"I'm so tired any alcohol will put me under the table."

There could be worse places.

"Bring us what Chef poured for everyone at the staff meeting today, Cecil. It's non-alcoholic, Cinna."

"The Taunton cider. Excellent choice, sir. I'll send your waiter over with it shortly." Bowing, the young man left them.

He watched Cinna twist in her chair and survey the room.

"It looks like an English inn. At least what I'd imagine one to be. I haven't been over there to check it out myself."

He nodded. "That was our intent. We're going to be trying some additions to the menu tonight. We've done well with the Dover sole and roast beef, but Chef has developed some new entrees."

She nodded, the flickering lights of the fire illuminating her face.

"Sometimes it's trial and error getting a business

off the ground."

"I guess I was naïve about everything that starting a business entailed. Maybe Magdalena and I both were. I thought it was pretty much finding a place, getting the menu set up, and opening the doors. I didn't think about things like negotiating a lease, ordering linens and cleaning supplies, getting menus and invoices printed, meeting health code regulations." She rolled her eyes.

He nodded. "It can be a 24/7 job."

"Well, things may be getting easier. One of the girls Mags used to dance with at the Silver Strike is off on maternity leave and is going to start coming in to help so we may actually get a day off now and then. Running the shop is more than brewing tea and waiting tables. There's bookkeeping, product development, ordering, advertising that has to be taken care of."

He moved back as their waiter arrived with a crystal carafe and two goblets. The liquid was the color of old gold as he poured for them.

He shook his head as the waiter produced menus.

"We're just going to try the Chef's new dishes tonight."

"Very good, sir. I'll check with the kitchen."

Cinna picked up her glass as he raised his.

"So what shall we drink to?" she asked.

"How about success?" That could encompass a variety of meanings. For the past couple years, it'd had to do with building his career. Since finding Cinnamon Smith again, his priorities had shifted.

She smiled and touched her glass to his.

The cider was as he remembered—like a chill breeze through a ripe orchard.

Cinna put her drink down, her cheeks flushing.

"What do you think?" he asked.

"It's great. Not like the stuff from the supermarket. Definitely meant for sipping slowly though. A little on the tart side."

He nodded, watching as she sat back and relaxed in her chair, one hand loose on the table. In the warmth from the fireplace, her eyelids drifted shut, her lashes feathered on her cheekbones. There were shadows under her eyes he usually didn't see in the morning. It looked like she had lost weight. Maybe she and her partner both had. Starting up a business from scratch wasn't easy in Vegas, especially for a couple of first-timers. Competition was cutthroat, even for a one-of-a-kind tea bar. If Jim McMasters were willing to give them a standing order, maybe things would ease up a little. Faint lines of fatigue webbed her eyes as her head shifted and her breathing softened. His palm itched to cover her hand with his own.

The noise of the food cart rolling up as their waiter arrived made her start, her eyes popping open. He acted as if he hadn't noticed.

"Lancashire hot pot, shepherd's pie." The waiter arranged the dishes family-style on the table. The china was embossed with the restaurant's intertwined C's. "Yorkshire pudding and Scottish smoked salmon with dill. Will there be anything else, sir?"

"I think this will do. Cinna?"

"I hope you're hungry, Tom." She shook her head.

"Can I serve you?"

"Please." She nudged her plate forward. "Just a little of everything."

He discovered he did have an appetite. Across the table, it appeared Cinna was hungry too as she let him give her seconds.

The chef came out to serve dessert personally from a heaping crystal bowl of trifle.

"It's too much." Cinna's pink tongue played with the dollop of whipped cream on her fork. "I can't tell you when I've eaten like this. Maybe the last time I was home for the holidays. Mags and I are pretty much into what's quick and fast."

Despite Vegas's reputation for fine dining, it didn't sound like there were a lot of dinner dates in her life.

"So when was the last time you saw everyone?" he asked.

Had he said something wrong? She was the one who had brought up the word home. She sat up reaching for her goblet, her fingers tightening around the stem as she looked away.

"Last Christmas, we were all together. Sage had to leave the day after to prepare for an appearance before a committee on a research grant he was up for. Then Mom and Dad were here in February for a quick weekend to celebrate their anniversary."

Her parents, Sage. No mention of Rosemary. Over the years, he'd wondered how he could apologize for just taking off the way he had. Maybe it was better he'd never gotten the chance. Surely a girl like Rosemary would have long forgotten him.

She pushed her dessert plate away.

"Any suggestions?"

"It was all great. Well, maybe, the cream sauce on the Yorkshire pudding had too much horseradish for me, but I'm probably being picky. You didn't see me refuse a lot."

"Glad you like it. Oh, Kyle."

Their waiter had returned to collect the dishes.

"Would you have someone bring the Jag around? I think we're done here." As much as he might wish to extend the evening, tomorrow would be another long workday for her.

"The Jag?" She cocked her head and looked at him curiously.

"Not mine, strictly a loaner. It's a 1959 XK, the old-time classic car. Jim keeps several one of a kind, top-notch cars for senior staff and our preferred players. We have a Bentley too. He says it makes a good impression for the Imperial. I have something a little more downscale for running around." He took a last sip of his water and rose to get her chair.

The silver XK was under the awning gathering admiring glances from passers-by. The doorman got the door for her as she sank into the leather seat, wiggling her way down.

"I only wish I lived farther away so I could enjoy the ride longer." She smiled over at him.

"It's a beauty. So where do you live?"

She gave him an address off downtown, not the best neighborhood.

"Mags and I usually just walk to work if we don't have stuff to carry. With the price of gas and finding parking, it's usually easier."

"I could manage a guest pass for you in our parking garage, if that would help. So you two have been living together since you came out here?"

"Right. It's a one-bedroom place we found after we rented the shop. We trade off using the bedroom and the couch. This is an expensive city so we've been trying to keep expenses down. We furnished it from thrift shops." As he got her door, she craned her neck and looked up at the darkened building. Spanish-style stucco, the roof was missing some of its red tiles. "Looks like she's not home yet."

"Why don't I swing by your store and see if she's ready to leave? It's not that far away."

"Well…" Cinna bit her lip. "She usually just gets a cab at this hour."

"It's no trouble." He followed her into the building and waited as she found her key.

"Okay, well then, thank you, Tom, that's kind of you. And thank you for dinner. It was great." She extended her hand.

Evidently, that was going to be it. No chaste goodnight kiss.

He squeezed her palm, feeling the fingers under his for a moment.

"My pleasure. Hope everything turns out well with your company this weekend."

Chapter Four

Magdalena had her hair wrapped in a towel as she emerged from the bathroom.

"Your turn," she said, bending over to dry her heavy, dark hair.

"Thanks. So did you hear from David Witheroe last night?"

"Sure did. I would have told you about it when I got in, but you were sacked out on the couch, dead to the world, when your date brought me home."

"Tom was not my date," Cinna emphasized. "This banquet he's taking me to is strictly business since he is, as he so eloquently put it, between girlfriends."

"Yeah, well with a ride like that I'd be tempted to mix business with pleasure if I thought he had a thing for tall, brunette ex-showgirls."

"Please be my guest."

"Actually, my current fantasy has a killer New Zealand accent. We talked for quite a while. The closer he gets, the closer I want him. Don't raise your eyebrows at me. You know how long it's been for both of us."

"Who's reminding whom about business?"

"Speaking of which my dream date is bringing along some special white and green teas for us he's really excited about. I love a man who can talk about flavonoids." Magdalena straightened and ran her hands through her hair.

"There still have to be limits as to what we'll do for business."

"Barbara Anthony called last night." Magdalena went over to stand with her back to the window, lifting her hair off the nape of her neck in the sunlight.

"How's she getting along with the twins?"

"Super. They're weaned, even trying to sit up, and she's ready to leave them for a while. Stan has the day off today and she's going to let him have some quality daddy-time with the twosome and come into the shop for us this afternoon. We need to do some major shopping, girl. We're in a time crunch."

"Oh, Mags. I could…I could just…" Her voice trailed off as Magdalena stared at her disbelieving.

"You could what? Wear a clean apron to the awards dinner? Wouldn't that make them sit up and take notice?"

Magdalena carried her towel into the bathroom, returning with her blow dryer and round brush. "Cinnamon, the Las Vegas Hospitality Industry Association banquet is a big deal. Very big. Millions of dollars hang on getting these awards. For the Imperial, it could be the breakout event. You and your date, kind-of date, semi-date, whatever, are going to be photographed, scrutinized, and evaluated up the ying-yang. You need to be the drop-dead, gorgeous, young business woman on the rise we both know you can be."

"Sounds drop-dead expensive," she muttered as Magdalena plugged in her dryer.

"What?" Magdalena started the dryer and ran her fingers through her bangs.

"Money." She scratched her palm.

"Well, I've got the names of some places off the Strip to try." Magdalena rolled up a section of her hair and dried it. "We'll scout out the whole package—dress, shoes, accessories…classy, lacy things."

"Oh, no, we won't, Magdalena. Tom isn't getting anywhere near any classy, lacy things. Forget about that."

"It's part of the package. Trust me. I want you to be the seducer out there. You need to project an image that will have those people panting for a good cup of tea."

"I don't think people in this town are going to connect lace undies with a good cup of tea."

"We'll see. Anyway, there was one more call." Her roommate turned down the dryer and scrunched her curls. "Another Smith girl has hit Sin City."

"Rosemary got in?"

"The one and only. She and her boyfriend…Ned, Jed, Ted? I was in swoon mode dreaming of David when I picked up her call. Had just checked into their hotel. They're staying at the Cote d'Azur. She didn't know their schedule, but she said she'd call back later."

"Oh, great." Life was getting complicated. Over the past few years, her sister's life had been taken up with dental school, a post-graduate internship, and setting up her own practice. Now if Rose had a man in her life, she might be more interested in him than what was going on with her kid sister. And with her hotel on the strip, she was safely away from Fremont Street, the Imperial, and Tom.

"Well, there's a world out there awaiting their morning caffeine. I'm going to get dressed and go on in. Take your time here."

"I won't be long." Cinna stood and found the throw pillows, tossing them back on the couch and disguising its use as a bed again.

"Should be an easy day with Barbara coming in. We'll take off, grab lunch somewhere, and find an outfit to make Tom forget he ever knew Rosemary."

Going on into the small bedroom with its adjoining bath, Cinna shook her head. She'd lain awake last night thinking about Tom's parting remark until she realized he'd been talking about the arrival of their tea scout.

Forget he knew Rosemary? If only it worked both ways.

****

The expression on Magdalena's face mirrored her own.

"No, yes?"

"Yes, no." Her partner shook her head. "The trouble with knock-offs is that it looks like you're trying hard to be hip."

"Yeah, I don't want to be a *wanna be*." Cinna sighed and returned to the dressing room to wiggle out of possibility number seventeen.

"So how did the outfit work for you?" The young sales clerk had returned to where Magdalena was gathering their things as she emerged.

"Thank you, but we'll think about it. We're still gathering ideas." She collected her purse from Magdalena.

"It's really hot. I don't know how long we'll have it in stock. DeAnna Davis was photographed just the other day in a dead-ringer for it," the salesclerk called after them.

"How about it? You could have the paparazzi

chasing you." Magdalena held the door for her as they emerged back into the afternoon heat.

"Yeah, what's her latest claim to fame? Being arrested twice in one night?"

"Right. You know…" Magdalena paused at the curb, tilting her head and wrinkling her brow. "Maybe we need to try a different approach. Something less au courant."

"Maybe *the* Dress isn't out there. Maybe I should just find something that fits and call it a day."

"Not so fast. I have an idea. Let's head back north. There's a shop on Fremont, out of this high rent craziness. I haven't been inside, but I've admired their windows. It's called VinTauge."

"I know where it is, but isn't it secondhand, used stuff, Mags? Like you said, this hospitality association banquet is a big deal." What enthusiasm she'd started with was ebbing away. "I mean I don't really want to wear someone else's castoffs."

"Trust me. It's upscale recycled designer duds. C'mon, girl. It's worth a try. If nothing else, it'll be fun to look and we'll be back close to the shop again."

Magdalena found a pen and a copy of their take-out menu in her purse as they exchanged the monorail for the bus.

"I probably have enough make-up left over from my days at the Strike to fix you up Saturday, but we'll need hair stuff." Turning the menu over, she started a list.

"Mags, there isn't enough conditioner in Las Vegas to tame this mop." Cinna shook her head sending her curls flying.

"Not trying to. I figure Tom likes you the way you

are. Don't look at me that way." Magdalena stared back at her. "We just need to glam you up a bit."

"Tom's only interested in having a female on his arm."

"Honey, if he's male, conscious, and breathing, he's interested in more than that. Nylons, not nylons." Magdalena bit her lip debating. "With us working inside pretty much 24/7 neither of us has much color. Maybe we can pick up a bronzer too. Tanned legs, a pair of open-toed stilettos."

"Come on, I don't wear heels, let alone fancy ones. I'll walk in and fall on my face. Won't that stop people in their tracks?"

"Tom will be there to catch you. Okay, this is our stop. Once more into the breech, girlfriend."

Cinna followed her down the steps and onto the sidewalk. Even with a break for lunch and a pick-me-up cocktail, the afternoon seemed long. The sun was lowering in the sky. Surely, Barbara would be glancing at her watch and thinking about getting home soon. She stopped short. Magdalena stood transfixed in front of a store window as passers-by made their way around her.

"Isn't it divine?" She drew a shaky breath and pointed a finger at a mannequin modeling a square-necked, black cocktail dress. "Cinna, Cinna, Cinna. Can't you just see Audrey Hepburn in that? Maybe with a big hat."

"Audrey, yes. Cinnamon, no." But Magdalena was pushing through the door, not listening to her.

The shop was nicer than she'd anticipated. Definitely an improvement on the used clothing shop she'd had in mind. Discreet racks stood on the polished bamboo floors under offset lighting. Something low and relaxing was playing on the store's sound system.

"Can I help you?" In a retro, double-breasted blue blazer, the young man seemed suitably attired.

"I love your window." Magdalena clasped her hands. "I've been past a number of times, but never stopped in."

"Thank you. Welcome to VinTauge. I'm Evan Kirkpatrick. My mother and a friend opened the store some years back as a venue to offer gently-used quality clothing. We do get a number of compliments on our windows. So how can I help you today?"

"It's for my friend here."

She looked up from the rack she'd been flipping through.

"Cinnamon is going to the annual awards dinner at the Convention Center this Saturday," Magdalena explained.

"Oh, the Las Vegas Hospitality Industry Association banquet. How special!"

"Yes, we know it's short notice."

"It's kind-of a last minute thing," she explained as the sales associate circled around, hand on chin studying her.

"Size eight, I'd venture."

"More like a ten usually."

"Go with the eight. We want to show off your curves, girl. So what do you think?" Magdalena asked. "I loved the dress in your window."

"Hm. Yes, it's quite nice. But…well, black is always classic, but it can be done to death, you know. I'm thinking…" He bit his lip before nodding decisively. "Yes, I have something that just came in. It's still in the back. Let me get it for you."

"Isn't this exciting? This is the place where we can find a one of a kind gown for you. Not a tartlet-starlet rip-off."

"Gown? Let's remember this is not a ball at the palace I'm going to."

She didn't like the way her friend snorted, but before she could say anything, Evan was back with something on a hanger.

For the first time in her life, her jaw actually sagged in shock as he held it out to them.

"Oh, Cinna." Magdalena moved over to pick up the dress with a tentative hand and let it drape over her fingers. "It's perfect. Talk about retro glamour."

"The blonde bombshell look," Evan assured her knowingly.

Blonde bombshell? Cinnamon Smith? When did those two things ever go together?

"Oh, Mags, that doesn't sound like me."

"Try it on. Just try it on. I want to see how you look in it. Do it, do it, do it, Cinna."

"I…" But Evan was taking her by the elbow over to one of the dressing rooms, hanging the hanger from a hook before he closed the louvered door.

Okay, well she could be a good sport. She kicked off her sandals, pulled off her T-shirt, and stepped out of her skirt as she contemplated the dress. The gold lamé sheath had slightly padded shoulders, elbow length sleeves, a V-neck and belted waist. The skirt split just above the knee, falling away in the back.

Probably worth more originally than she and Mags cleared in a week. She inhaled, stiffed her upper lip, and slid the dress over her head. It settled around her as she fastened the belt. The waist was snug, but not uncomfortable; the neckline low enough just to hint at something. She ran her hands through her curls to fluff them before emerging from the dressing room.

Evan's face broke into a smile as Magdalena stared at her wide-eyed.

"Well, va-va-voom, girl!"

****

She pushed the door open with one hand and held it for Magdalena. From the counter, Barbara looked up and waved a hand.

"Welcome back. How did it go?" she asked.

"Mission accomplished. We found the most fabulous dress at VinTauge, the classic resell shop over on Fremont. We left it there for alterations. So then, of course, we had to find some things to go with it, right?" Magdalena opened a bag. "A sparkly barrette, highlighting to glam up our princess—"

"Cinna does not stand for Cinderella."

"Close enough. Some dangly earrings to add interest, yes?"

"I love them!" Barbara reached out a hand.

"And, courtesy of Shoe World, the latest in glass slippers and matching clutch. Ta-da!" Magdalena produced the last items triumphantly.

"Well, you girls made out like bandits, didn't you?"

"So how were things here?" She circled the counter and hit the no sale button on the register to open the cash drawer. "Well!"

"Yeah, business was good. We had a number of people coming by to redeem these things." Barbara held up one of the coupons they had included in their gift bags for the Imperial. "And we had a big run on the tins

59

of tea you had over there." She pointed to an empty shelf.

Magdalena looked over at her. "That was our new Celestial Harmony blend, wasn't it?"

"Right. The guests at the hotel must really have liked it," she said.

"I looked in the back for more when we ran out, but I couldn't find. So I started a mailing list." Barbara picked up a paper from the counter and handed it to her. "We've got quite a few names."

"Sacramento, Portland, Port Arthur. Bar Harbor, Maine. Wow, Mags. We may really have a hit on our hands."

"They were adamant about getting more of it. Really, the men as well as the women." Barbara looked thoughtful. "It was kind of strange almost. I guess I didn't appreciate how into tea some people can be."

"We worked hard getting the balance of flavors correct. So everything went all right? Stan able to cope with things on the home front?"

"Aside from one panicked phone call about a missing binky, I think so. It ought to give him a little more appreciation for me anyway." Barbara took off her apron and stretched. At six feet something, she had played for UNLV on a basketball scholarship.

"You know, Cinna. I think we're out of the white sage I used in the celestial harmony blend. Maybe when David gets here, he can speed up a re-order for us. Did a David Witheroe call? Killer New Zealand accent? He's our tea scout, due to hit Vegas any time."

"No, but there were a couple others." Barbara picked up some slips of paper from beside the phone.

"This one was for you, Cinna, from your sister.

She's down at the Cote d'Azur. She asked about getting together there for lunch tomorrow." She held out a slip of paper.

"Thanks." She reached over to take it, thinking tomorrow might be all right. Meet somewhere on the Strip, safely away from downtown.

"The other was from Tom Marco. I think he said he was calling from the Imperial. It was a little confusing."

She raised her head to look at Barbara, wrinkling her forehead as she studied the paper in her hand.

"He asked for you, Cinna, and then to speak to Magdalena. I'm not sure what he wanted. He sounded tongue-tied when I said you'd both be out for the day. I got the feeling it was something important. Anyway, he said he'd call back tomorrow."

"Damn." Magdalena froze in the act of running the cash register tape and looked over at her, grimacing. "Geez, I hope he isn't going to cancel after we did all that shopping. Well, don't look like that, girlfriend. At least if he does, it isn't like we broke the bank."

That wasn't exactly what she was feeling.

Chapter Five

"Another guy." Magdalena hung up the phone and looked down at the pad she'd been writing on. "He was calling from Eau Claire, Wisconsin."

"Let me guess. He wants to order the celestial harmony tea," Cinna said.

"ASAP. He said someone he knew, who'd been here a couple days ago, had told him about it. He's even willing to pay for expedited shipping." She stopped and pursed her lips. "I'll tell you, Cinna. It was a more than a little odd. He was talking under his breath the whole time like he didn't want anyone to hear him."

"Odd doesn't even begin to describe this whole thing. When was the last time we had a run on tea like this?"

"Like nev—" The phone interrupted her.

"Good morning, SpecialTeas, the great way to begin your day. How may I help you? Oh, yes." Magdalena arched her eyebrows and widened her eyes at Cinna as she reached for her scratchpad.

Well, maybe this was another step on their climb toward profitability. She glanced at the clock again. She'd gotten hold of Rose last night and they agreed to meet in the lobby of Rose's hotel at one. She'd managed to deflect her sister's interest in coming downtown to see the shop by telling her they were up to their neck in remodeling.

With a little luck, Rosemary's convention would be over in a few days and she'd be back on her way to the windy city to improve the smiles of Chicago-land citizens while avoiding crossing paths with trouble in Las Vegas.

Speaking of which, she handed back a customer's change and looked up as the temple chimes tinkled. It was just another one of their morning regulars though. Usually Tom was here by this time, typically swinging by on his way into work. She drummed her fingers on the counter.

"Problem?" Magdalena asked as she steered a cart through the connecting door from the back.

"Just wondering where he is and what's going on?"

"Probably on the road. The last I heard he was planning on being here sometime Saturday."

Cinna stared at her friend. "I thought I'd see him before then."

"Him who? Girl, who are we talking about?"

"Tom. Barbara Anthony said he called about something yesterday."

"Oh, right. I was thinking of David Witheroe, my fantasy, not yours."

"Tom is not my fantasy. I just want to know what it was he—"

"Whatever. Look alive, girlfriend. Twelve o'clock."

There was a line between Tom's brows as he made his way to where they were, his suit jacket hanging open.

Magdalena raised a hand in greeting.

"I'm sorry we were out. Barbara said you called yesterday." Cinna steadied herself on the counter. She

63

suddenly felt as chilled as the marble surface. Tom looked serious.

"Cinna, I'm going to clean the tea press."

"Actually…" Tom swiveled around surveying the tearoom. A punk couple with pink and purple spiked hair was finishing a pot of tea and Dundee cake at one table. "I'd like to talk to the both of you if you have the time."

"Okay." She looked over at Magdalena. "We're free right now."

"Sure. Why don't we sit down?" Magdalena led the way to a table in the corner and waited as Tom pulled out chairs for them. Usually, he sat at the counter when he came in. Balanced now on one of their ornate wrought-iron chairs, he seemed out-of-place. He hesitated a minute before clasping his hands loosely on the table and drawing a breath.

"It's a…I wanted to talk to you about the samples of tea you brought over to the hotel the other day."

"So did you like them?" Cinna asked slowly. Something didn't feel right. Her sense of unease was growing. Magdalena was chewing her lip as she looked at Tom.

"Barbara said we had a number of guests from the Imperial coming in yesterday, redeeming the coupons we included in the gift bags and asking about one of our teas."

"I bet I can guess which one. We had some comments on it."

"The Celestial Harmony blend. So did people like it?" Magdalena asked.

"Well, probably. Or appreciated it. We did have one guest who seemed to have a problem."

"What?" She looked over Magdalena who was staring at Tom, looking as puzzled as she felt.

"It was a lady, one of the contestants in the darts tournament we've been running as a special promotion this week. She and her husband traveled here from the U.K. where she's a nationally ranked player. It seems she missed her starting time for the finals and she was, ah…pretty much out of sorts about it."

"I don't… What does that have to do with us?" Cinna asked.

"She and her husband had been drinking the harmony blend and, well, they never made it out of their room and down to Draughts where we were holding the tournament."

"What? They slept through it?"

"Oh, my God!" Magdalena gasped. "Food poisoning. Oh, my Lord. Is that what you think?"

"No, not that. Well, not exactly." Tom raised his eyebrows and grimaced. "They were in bed, but not sick. I don't think. At least not in the usual sense."

They stared at him blankly.

"What are you talking about?" Cinna wished he would get to the point.

"I guess I'm asking if there is any way the harmony tea could be considered an aphrodisiac? If it has any other properties than the usual tea."

"An, an aphrodisiac? Are you nuts!" She turned to glare at Magdalena who was bent over, shrieking in laughter, covering her face with both hands.

"I'm only asking. It's just that the Wightmans had such a strong reaction. Not that he was complaining really, but Mrs. Wightman was. And some of the other guests." Tom shook his head slowly. "Delores said they were calling the desk with all kinds of questions. Then Brielle said the tea caddy on the breakfast buffet was almost cleaned out when I sent her to check."

"Well, it wasn't due to our tea," Cinna said hotly.

"It really wasn't." Magdalena straightened up wiping a finger under her eyes. "I wish we could claim credit. Romance in a teabag! Another way to get into hot water. Think of the advertising campaign we could have here in Vegas! Wow. But really Tom, Cinna and I worked on that blend ourselves for weeks."

"Weeks and weeks."

"It's a combination of a white tea, lychee blossoms, white sage for balancing, and a top note of rose petals. We've drunk it ourselves. Potfulls of it, adjusting the blend and never, never noticed the slightest, ah, oh my. Excuse me." Her partner reached for a napkin and blew her nose as she hiccupped.

At least someone thought it was funny. Suppose Mrs. What's-her-name decided to sue since she missed her tournament time because of their tea?

"We wouldn't be serving something to the public we didn't think was safe." Cinna knew her cheeks were flushed. "We drank the Celestial Harmony blend every day, didn't we, Mags?"

Magdalena nodded. "Maybe it's just being in Vegas. The power of suggestion along with relaxing, being away from home, enjoying a luxury suite, you know." She waved a hand. "Honestly, Tom, we probably tried it on you when we were working on it."

"Wow. Okay." He ducked his head, half hiding a grin. "Well, I thought it was pretty far out, but they aren't first-time visitors here and I guess the effect was, well, noticeable. I comped their stay and offered to pay the entry fees for next year's tournament for Celia so I think they're mollified."

"I'll get that." Magdalena got up to answer the phone. She watched as her friend shook her head and reached for her pen and pad.

"I'm sorry if we caused any trouble." She held herself up stiffly.

"I wouldn't say that, Cinna. I just wanted to give you a heads-up about some possible side effects." He moved his hand toward hers, stopping when she raised her head to glare at him.

"I know it sounds weird and even if it is true to some extent—"

"Which it isn't!"

"That some people were affected by it."

"Unfortunately, we're sold out of it, or I'd give you some to have analyzed."

"I think we may have some teabags back at the hotel. I had Brielle pull it off the buffet. Well, I need to get back to work." He pushed himself back from the table and stood slowly, looking down to where her hands were knotted on the table.

The door chimes sounded as a group of ladies entered.

"I won't take up any more of your time. Looks like you're getting busy. Hope the rest of your day goes better."

She straightened her fingers, working the kinks out as she watched him leave. It had to, didn't it?

****

The sliding glass doors parted soundlessly. She shoved the hair back out of her eyes as she marched across the blue and gold carpeted atrium toward the concierge desk. She could feel her lips still moving. She hadn't been able to stop off at the apartment to change before heading to the Strip. She'd wasted too much time arguing with Magdalena that there was no way the chemical combination of teas they'd used could produce any side effects like Tom had described. To say she was feeling grubby was putting it mildly. Something else that was Tom's fault. At the desk, a uniformed young woman looked up to smile and greet her.

"Hey, hold up a minute, stranger." A hand on her shoulder spun her around.

Tall, blonde, every cell devoted to producing the optimum in skin, hair, eyes, and figure, Rosemary Smith could stop people in their tracks. What else was new?

She stifled a sigh and managed a smile.

A group of boys pulling their suitcases toward the door stopped to stare. They weren't looking at her.

"Oh, hi, Rosemary."

"Oh, hi? Is that the best you can manage for your big sister? Sounds like you really missed me."

She was swept into a warm embrace tinged ever so slightly with expensive perfume.

"After almost a year. I can't believe the luck that this conference was scheduled out here in Las Vegas."

"Yeah, what are the chances?" That it would be held in the convention capital of the U.S.? "You look good."

"Thanks. I bought the greatest combination sunscreen and moisturizer the other day. I'll write the name down for you. The gal that owns the tanning booth in our building put me onto it."

"So how is Masterpiece Manor doing?" Dr. Rosemary Smith, D.D.S.'s practice was devoted to the best in dental enhancements—whitening, crowns, caps.

"Fabulous. Really taking off. I thought we could eat here in the Marseillaise Room. We had dinner there last night and it was wonderful."

With an arm around her shoulders, Rosemary guided her over to the restaurant entrance, her heels clicking on the marble floor. People made way for them, Rosemary gifting them with a smile. If the men had been wearing hats, they would have raised them.

"The practice is going great guns. I think we've found a niche that needed filling."

Was that dental humor?

Rose paused outside the restaurant entrance to read a menu posted on a stand beside a huge clay urn spilling orange and fuchsia blossoms.

"They have a great selection of seafood." Her sister ran a manicured finger down the page.

"It looks fine." As long as she skipped the shellfish which made her break out.

"This conference has been tremendous, Cinna. I've picked up tons of ideas on marketing and promotion as well as keeping a website fresh. The Internet is something you might think of using for your shop. You can ask a designer to come up with a website."

"It's something we've discussed. It's on our to-do list actually, but we've already so much going on now."

"Oh, yes, you'll have to tell me about the remodeling you're doing."

Remodeling. She winced.

Rosemary favored the hovering maître d' with a dazzling smile and waved across the room. "Thank you.

I have someone saving a table for us."

"So what did you think of the dental whitener I sent you for your birthday? Have you been using it regularly?"

"Oh, sure. I try to." She followed her sister, trim in knit, striped shirt and white tennis shorts. Well, she tried when she thought of it, in between running out the door to get SpecialTeas open on time, or collapsing in bed after twelve hours on her feet.

"Twice a day, Cinna, religiously. It's fabulous. One of my assistants tried it when she was over in Switzerland and noticed the improvement right away. It's completely natural. Even the bottle is biodegradable. Here we are."

At the table, a man was getting up from his seat. Probably on the other side of forty, he was slightly built with receding hair and glasses. Beside her sister no one would have noticed him. Rosemary gave him a mega-watt smile and held out a hand. He curled her fingers in his own.

"Cinna, I'd like you to meet Ed Dwyer. Ed, this is my sister, Cinnamon."

"One of the spice girls." He extended his hand for a firm handshake. "I'm so glad to meet you." He came around to hold her chair for her. "Rosie has told me so much about you."

Rosie?

"I admire your entrepreneurship in starting a new business venture out here." He moved over to help Rosemary with her chair.

"Ed's an OB/GYN from Lincoln Park."

She closed her eyes. She didn't want to think how they had met.

A waiter came over to fill their water goblets with his pitcher.

"Let me tell you about our specials today. Our feature today is a blackened…"

She sighed and listened politely as their waiter completed his recitation and left them.

"Ed's originally from Duluth, but he got his degree from the University of Chicago. His daughter has been granted early admission there." Rosemary flashed him the kind of smile featured in ads for her dental practice.

Well, no ring on his finger, or sign one had been recently removed.

"I understand your degree is in chemistry. So how did that lead to opening a tea emporium?" Rose's friend asked.

The brown eyes behind his glasses were warm. While he wasn't handsome, probably nearer her height than her sister's, he looked kind.

She drew a breath and began the saga of how a downturn in research grants lead to the loss of her job.

"And then my college friend Magdalena Kasas called with the idea of opening a tea bar here. She thought since I knew something about chemical processes and reactions, I might be able to help. It's Magdalena, though, who has the real know-how about tea, the educated palate and all. Anyway, I withdrew my 401K money and headed west."

Their waiter was back to take their orders. She chose a broiled sole while Rosemary selected a seafood salad and her companion got paella. After the morning they'd had, she didn't need to challenge her stomach with anything exotic.

"I know what you're saying about research money.

With the economic downturn, it's tightening up across the board."

"Last month, Ed and I ran a half-marathon to raise money for inner-city free clinics in Chicago."

Half-marathon? Rosemary? She wouldn't have put the two things together unless it involved raising money for poor children's dental work. Was this what love did to someone?

"So how are things going out here? Are you building a customer base?" Ed leaned forward, clasping his hands on the table. Rosemary looked interested.

"I don't know. I thought we were. At least…" She traced a design in the moisture beading on her glass.

"What? What is it, sis?"

"Oh, nothing. Just something came up today that might turn out to be a problem." She stared at the tablecloth.

"What? Tell me, Cinna."

"I don't want to bother you two…" She stopped to blink her eyes. *Drat.* It was all catching up to her. She balled up her fists, the nails cutting into her palms. Was she about to start crying?

"What's going on?" Rosemary exchanged concerned glances with Ed.

"It's just… It's so stupid. We had a complaint, or well, I don't know. Maybe a concern. About one of our products."

"What happened?"

"Oh." She tilted her head back and took a breath. How to explain it without mentioning someone's name? "A hotel near us asked us to bring them some special sample gift sets of our teas. We were hoping if they liked our products, they'd give us a standing order. So

Magdalena and I made up these fancy little bundles with a variety of our teas and a coupon good at the shop. We included two of the new Celestial Harmony teabags we had recently developed."

"Okay."

"It is a combination of a white tea and lychee blossoms. Lychee blossoms produce a heart-shaped fruit with a slight honey-like flavor. We use the blossoms along with a white sage for balancing and add rose petals as a top note. We tested the tea in various combinations, like we always do, until we felt it was right. Believe me, we drank gallons of the stuff for weeks."

"But there was a problem with it? Something happened at the hotel?"

"Did someone have an allergic reaction?" Ed asked.

"No. Well, maybe they think they did. One lady was in town to play in some stupid darts tournament the hotel was hosting. Only she missed competing because she claims she was affected by drinking our tea."

"Food poisoning? She got sick?"

"No." Cinna covered her face and bowed her head. "She and her husband were in bed, but apparently not um…well…resting."

"Excuse me, madam. Your order." She moved aside as the waiter delivered their plates and did something with his pepper mill.

Rosemary stared at her making no attempt to pick up her silverware.

"And are they complaining?" Ed looked like he was trying not to laugh.

Rosemary shot him a look. "Cinna is upset about

this. You aren't taking this seriously, are you?"

"No. Well, I don't know. Things have been a little crazy. Mags and I were out of the shop yesterday afternoon. The gal who covered for us said there was a steady stream of people from the hotel coming in and buying up all the harmony blend we had in stock. And, apparently, the news has made it onto the Internet because now we're getting orders and phone calls from all over the country."

"So what did the hotel say?" Rosemary speared a fat shrimp with her fork.

Yeah, the hotel. Be careful there.

"The manager was in this morning asking about it. He wasn't mad, I guess. Just asking about side effects. They'd had a number of curious questions from some of their guests. He'd already pulled the rest of the tea from their breakfast buffet."

"Wow. What do you think, Ed?"

Her friend had been listening quietly. He reached for a bread stick in the basket, broke it, and dipped one end in his paella. Chewing slowly, he seemed lost in thought.

"It's interesting." He shook his head and smiled. "Rose petals, lychee blossoms and white tea."

"And white sage, but nothing we don't use every day in a variety of teas."

"Right, but There's a well-known medical experiment that has been duplicated with the same results a number of times that may have something to do with it." Ed took a sip of his water. "Pictures of women have been shown to groups of men who are then asked to rate them on a scale of attractiveness and desirability. Consistently, the pictures of women taken at the height of their reproductive cycles are judged most desirable. The results have been duplicated time and again."

"So what do you think might have happened?" Rosemary asked.

Ed shrugged. "Understand I'm just hypothesizing. But if the relaxing benefits of the tea coincided with the peak doctors call the Venus week, male hormones could be stimulated generating the desire to reproduce. When estrogen levels are high, women are more confident, socially active, and at ease. Testosterone peaks during this week too and so, a strong desire for intimacy occurs. Add in an attractive partner, being in Vegas on vacation, and well, sparks could fly."

Cinna swallowed. Her lunch, untouched on her plate, looked less appetizing than ever.

"Wow. Cinna, you and Magdalena may have really stumbled onto something."

Ed nodded. "And, of course, if you and your friend didn't happen to be in the right part of your cycles and weren't involved in a relationship, you probably wouldn't have noticed anything."

Their waiter picked up Rosemary's glass to refill it. He was probably hearing more about human biology than he wanted to.

She certainly was.

Chapter Six

Hands on hips, he stopped and surveyed the floor area. It was a time in the day when things were winding down. There'd be a lull during the lunch break before the action picked up again.

In the pits, the table games were grouped together. Blackjack, craps, and the roulette wheel were still drawing crowds while it looked like the poker tables were breaking up. Even so, business looked good. And it hadn't been like their dealers were complaining about idle tables or the size of the tips customers left since the Imperial's opening. It made the shortfall in their revenues even more inexplicable. He shook his head.

At one of the blackjack tables, Ron Caisson had his arm around a player. From the size of the man's chip stack, it was evident he'd had a successful outing. Ron was signaling one of the cocktail servers. Comping the winner some champagne? It looked like he was marking the player's club card too. It was the way the casino monitored player's bets and time at the tables. Raising the player's credit marker? He winced. It was probably justifiable. Still he wished Ron would check with the casino host first. But then he also wished Ron would clock in on time and cut out leaving early.

"Oh, Mr. Marco!"

He turned to see Brielle Bennett, trim in her Imperial Hotel blazer and navy skirt, hurrying his way down the hall.

"I'm sorry to bother you." Despite probably being closer to thirty than twenty with her oversized glasses, brown eyes, and slight lisp, Brielle always reminded him of one of their teenage-aged spa attendants or lifeguards rather than a member of the management team.

"It's okay. I was just on my way back to the construction site to see how the addition is coming along before I grab some lunch. What's going on?"

"Mr. McMasters asked me if I could track you down. You know how he hates to use cell phones or the pagers."

He grinned. "Just doesn't seem quite polite to interrupt someone in that fashion, does it now?" He'd spent so much time with the older gentleman over the past few years it was like the Imperial's Chairman of the Board was wired into his head.

Brielle nodded. "Mr. McMasters is in the Exeter Club with a guest he'd like you to meet. Someone who's here from England, I think."

"Okay, sure. Thank you, Brielle."

Other men might have watched Brielle leave, but he bit his lip, changing direction and thinking. Celia Wightman? Was she still miffed about the harmony tea incident? He thought he had smoothed things over with her. Was she upset enough to want to complain to Gentleman Jim? He hoped not. It wouldn't help Cinna and Magdalena's tea business if McMasters got the idea there were problems with their products.

The Exeter Club had been Jim McMasters's pet project. A take on a London gentleman's club, it was situated in the rear of the mezzanine. Employee positions here were some of their highest bid openings. Its suite of rooms included a book-lined lounge area where a pianist played quietly in the corner. Other rooms in the suite included alcoves for Jim's beloved whist and snooker as well as private gaming areas for the high limit baccarat, black jack, roulette, and card games their preferred players sought. The Club's inclusion in the Imperial's renovation had been part of re-positioning the hotel as a small, exclusive luxury destination and it had brought with it a not inconsequential outlay of capital. Fortunately, they were beginning to see return in the type of clientele they were targeting.

He made his way to the back where floor to ceiling windows looked out onto the rooftop garden. It was Gentleman Jim's favorite place at the Imperial, providing a respite from the hotel's daily bustle. As he stepped through the French doors to the garden, he could see McMasters's profile turned toward someone in a lounge chair under a striped umbrella.

He inhaled and paused to breath in the fragrance of the desert blossoms the horticultural staff cultivated. In spite of the sunshine and slight breeze, as well as a cloudless sky overhead, McMasters looked tense as he looked up.

It wasn't Celia Wightman. McMasters's companion put her cocktail glass on the table and looked up expectantly, taking off her sunglasses. Probably a contemporary of Gentleman Jim's, she looked like the classic English gentlewoman with her fair complexion, light blue eyes, and pearls.

"Thomas." Gentleman Jim sounded relieved at his appearance. "I'm so glad you could join us. Elspeth, this is Thomas Marco, our general manager here at the Imperial, my good right hand, and the one responsible for all the splendid changes we've made to the property."

He started to protest, but McMasters didn't give him a chance.

"And Thomas, this is my dear, old, old… Of course, I mean in length of acquaintance, my most dear and valued friend, Elspeth Porter-Hayes, sister of a flight mate of mine, Gordon McAlister. Elspeth has come all the way from Manchester with a friend to see the Imperial."

He took the hand Mrs. Porter-Hayes extended. Soft and well kept, it looked as if she habitually wore gloves. He bowed over it.

"Quite a trip. Thank you for giving us a try."

"Well, my friend Joyce was coming this way. Her grandchildren live in San Francisco so I more or less invited myself along to see how things were going out here."

"Oh, quite, yes, yes. Lovely surprise. I was entirely taken aback when the girls popped in this morning." There was a note he didn't recognize in McMaster's voice. He turned to look at his employer.

"You see Elspeth is one of our investors, part of the consortium back in the U.K."

All right. That put things in a different light.

He took his time seating himself in the chair McMasters was indicating while Gentleman Jim's guest reclaimed her drink and sunglasses.

"I see. Nice to meet you. Is this your first trip to the States?"

"Oh, no. My husband and I visited the east coast a

number of times, but I've never been so far west. Then Joyce rang up to tell me about her holiday to visit family in California and did I want to come along? So I thought, what a jolly idea to pop in and surprise James."

"I've shown Elspeth and her chum around a bit."

"Joyce is off in the baccarat room now having a go at it. James, the pictures you've sent back to Britain don't do the property justice."

"Thank you. So kind of you to say, my dear."

"So how long can you spend with us?" Tom asked.

"Just over the weekend, then we'll be traveling on. I thought I'd drop in, look things over for the other investors, you know. Give everyone a personal report when I get back. Your latest quarterly report from the accounting firm should be out now, shouldn't it?" Mrs. Porter-Hayes smiled at her old friend.

Quarterly report. Did that explain the clear signals of unease he was getting from McMasters?

He nodded. "Yes." He drug the word out. "We have the preliminary figures, but the final report hasn't been delivered yet."

And it technically hadn't. Although he'd seen it at the auditors' office in Henderson, the bound, printed copy hadn't been mailed to the Imperial. However, the accountants' initial findings and their finalized reports had never differed significantly.

"Oh, yes, well, I thought I'd just give it a look-see while I was over here, you know." Gentleman Jim's guest sipped her drink. "So tasty, James. Can I treat myself to another one of these? What did you call it?"

"A Margarita. Of course, my dear." McMasters raised his hand at a passing waiter and pointed at Mrs. Porter-Hayes' glass. "Elspeth is quite the math wizard,

Thomas. A degree from Cambridge, worked for Her Majesty's Inland Revenue, O.B.E. for service to the crown. Right, dear girl?"

McMasters's eyes met his own. They weren't happy. He wondered if his boss could keep Mrs. Porter-Hayes's Margarita glass filled.

****

"You're squishing," Magdalena complained. "Spread those piggies." She sat back on her heels and contemplated Cinna's feet.

"I think we need a darker shade, you know." She held up her bottle of polish and frowned at it. "This Slice of Watermelon doesn't do it for me."

"Do you really think anyone is going to be paying attention to my feet, Mags?" She wiggled as new cotton balls were pushed between her toes.

"It's part of the whole package, Cinna. Like the new lingerie we picked up at Bare Necessities."

The lace-trimmed, ivory teddy had cost more than her high school prom dress.

"We want you to feel beautiful, alluring. You are going to be up against some major hitters looks-wise, and we want eyes to be on you. Keep your hands in that soaking solution. I'll work on shaping and buffing when I get done down here. I'm going to try this Strawberry Sherbet the gal at the beauty shop recommended." She reached over to pick up another bottle of polish and shake it. "It's what I'll use on your nails, too."

"Are there any colors not food related?"

"Makes you wonder, doesn't it? The hair highlighting kit we picked out is called Vanilla Honey."

"Yum. So, do I mention Ed's theory to Marco? I

81

mean it was just a guess," she asked.

"From a doctor who ought to know what he's talking about." Magdalena stopped what she was doing to look up. "How well does Rosemary know him? I mean you don't suppose he's her—"

"I didn't ask." Cinna shuddered. "Her judgment about men has had to get better since those days with Tom."

"Let's be fair to the man. Tom didn't actually accuse us of anything. But, Cinna, something must have happened. I mean it's not a thing people would normally talk about and plant the idea in other couples' minds. You know, a group hysteria type of situation. I don't think it's our fault, but on the other hand, we probably better not sell any more of the Celestial Harmony before thinking all this through. Maybe David Witheroe will have an idea. We can talk to him about it when he's here. Oh, yes." Magdalena bit her lip and studied the results of her efforts. "Most satisfactory, don't you think?"

"Sure, fine."

"It's not like Tom is going to be on the hook for child support. Hey!" Magdalena's head came up to stare at her as she jerked her foot away.

"That was a joke, Cinna. I can't see anyone suing the Imperial or us because they fooled around without being careful."

"Sorry, just nerves."

"Tom should be in tomorrow morning for his usual fill-up. You probably ought to say something to him."

Great—tea, an order of shortbread, and a comparison of her and Magdalena's reproductive cycles with those of his randy guests.

****

Business seemed better than usual.

He stood in line behind half a dozen customers. Most of the small circular tables in front were filled while other shoppers perused the shelves and display areas. A regular in the corner was busy on his laptop. Behind him, he heard the sound of the door chimes as someone else entered.

Cinna was taking orders while her friend filled them. The pair typically worked in sync, but today their timing was off. Cinna seemed distracted in contrast to Magdalena's brisk cheerfulness.

He worked his way up behind a pot of jasmine tea and a whole-grain muffin.

"Just the usual today. A large Breakfast Blend, leaded."

She nodded, attempting a smile that didn't quite reach her eyes. She was counting out his change when Magdalena put his order on the counter and paused.

"I can take over here, Cinna, if you want a moment with Tom."

Ordinarily, that would have sounded promising except for the marked signals of reluctance he was getting from Cinnamon.

"Sure, thanks. Do you have some time? I don't want to make you late to work," Cinna asked. She twisted her fingers.

"It's okay. Dolores should be there and Brielle Bennett usually comes in early." He folded a bill in half and stuck it in the tip jar. A good thing since her boss, Ron Caisson, was chronically late.

"Maybe we can have a seat." She nodded at a nearby table.

He followed her over and sat down sipping his drink. He watched as she took a breath, smoothing out wrinkles in her apron.

He waited.

"It's…well, I wanted to talk to you about, about what you came in for yesterday. You know about the side effects…possible, unintentional side effects of our house Celestial Harmony blend." She bit her lower lip, her shoulders sagging.

"I didn't mean to upset the two of you. I just wondered if you knew about any added benefits from the tea."

"No! Well, not us. That is Magdalena and me. But then yesterday I was talking to a doctor, an OB/GYN." She looked away. "And he had some thoughts, a theory about what could have happened."

He waited as she drew a less than steady breath, balling her fists up on the table.

"There might be a medical explanation? You've stumbled onto an herbal V—?"

"I guess there have been studies where men can tell when women are at the peak of their reproductive cycles." Cinna swallowed hard, staring at the table. "Men can pick it out from pictures they're shown and they judge these women as the most attractive and desirable."

He sat back, regarding her.

"Anyway, this M.D. thought that if the relaxing part of the Celestial Harmony Blend was combined with being on vacation in Vegas…and then if all that coincided with the optimum point of a woman's cycle." Her voice slowed. "It could stimulate everyone's hormones and…" She waved a limp hand and looked away.

"Put people in the mood. Wow!" He gave a low whistle.

"Yeah, well." She looked up at him. Fatigue shadowed her eyes as if she hadn't been sleeping. Under the circulating fan, a stray curl escaped her headband to tickle her cheek.

"I don't know if it's even a problem. Like I said except for Mrs. Wightman, no one complained. You could be sitting on a gold mine. You might want to consider re-naming it though.' He raised an eyebrow and smiled.

"David Witheroe, our tea scout, is due to arrive sometime today. He's an absolute expert on tea. He's hitching rides across the country so his schedule isn't really set. Maybe he'll know something about it."

"Hitchhiking during a Nevada summer?" He shook his head. "Brave man."

"Magdalena said he told her it's his favorite way to see the country and meet people. When he gets here, we can ask him about the tea blend. Find out if he's ever experienced, well not personally experienced himself, but um…" Her cheeks flushed. "Heard about side effects, consequences of a combination like ours."

Flustered, her cheeks pink, she looked more like the young girl he'd known in Des Moines a dozen years ago than the more than occasionally harried co-owner of a new business.

"So how long have you been working with him?" Maybe she'd relax if they talked about other things.

"Ever since we opened. He sends us newsletters and sample packs of things he's run across along with his shipments. We order through a website operated by his sister in New Zealand."

"Tea scout dot com?"

"Something like that." She drew a breath and glanced toward the front where chimes were announcing the arrival of customers. "I better get back to work and let you get to your job, too."

"Sure." He stood and pulled back her chair. Standing close, her head was near his chest, her ash-blonde curls tumbling back as she looked up.

"About Saturday night. How would six-thirty work to pick you up? Cocktails are from seven to eight with the dinner afterward."

"Six-thirty sounds fine." She smiled as she moved past him, the fragrance of jasmine, vanilla, and ginger trailing after her. She didn't seem as if she were looking forward to it as much as he was, but at least her parting smile had been more genuine than the first one she'd given him today.

Chapter Seven

It had to be him. As she let herself in, two dark heads were bent over the counter deep in conversation. Neither seemed to have noticed the door chimes.

She cleared her throat.

Magdalena's head snapped back and the figure beside her straightened up.

And up. And up.

Six-eight? Six-ten? Seven-feet?

Automatically, she held out her hand, her jaw dropping. In pictures from his newsletters, he'd always dwarfed the tea growers he was standing beside, but she'd assumed that was because they were really short. Maybe not so much.

"Magdalena found me here on your doorstep, took pity on me, and let me in." The accent didn't come from anywhere within a thousand miles of Las Vegas.

She had never seen anything that looked less like a lost puppy.

"I got into town about midnight. Got a lift from a lorry driver out of Carson City. Found a place to doss down and woke up early this morning. Did a bit of a walkabout, you know. Found Magdalena here, keys to the kingdom in her hand. David Witheroe at your service. Cinnamon Smith, I presume."

She nodded as he squeezed her fingers and beamed down at Magdalena who seemed oblivious to the fact she was even there. Six-ten easily with a head of unruly black hair, dark eyes, and a smile even Rosemary couldn't help but approve; there wasn't a fat cell on his body. Maybe scaling the Himalayas and walking across most of the Indian sub-continent had that effect.

"David, how nice to finally meet you. We've been looking forward to meeting you in person. I see Magdalena found something for you."

At the sound of her name, her partner's face turned toward her blankly.

"Ah, yes, this." David raised his mug. "Capital. A green tea blend with an interesting top note." He took a sip, rolling it around in his mouth. "Yes, I think jasmine with perhaps a soupçon of lemongrass, dare I say?"

What the heck was a soupçon? She hadn't encountered it in any of the scientific measurements back in college.

"That's it. It's one we developed last winter, didn't we, Mags?" *Get into this conversation.* Her roommate was acting as stunned as she'd been when Tom had asked her out.

Magdalena smiled.

"I'm…ah, I'll go get things started up in the back so we're ready for our morning. You can stay out here and talk to David." Like Magdalena needed to have her arm twisted.

Cinna paused in the act of pushing open the connecting door to the kitchen. The grassy, smoky odor of the Brazilian yerba mate they had roasted the day before still hung in the air. Behind her, Magdalena and David were already bent over the counter again deep in tea talk. She shook her head. Somehow she didn't think tea was what her friend was interested in today.

She found a clean apron in the closet and used the mirror in the restroom to secure her curls back with a barrette. Adding water to the potpourri pot, she studied the row of simmering fragrances.

"Well, well, well." She picked up a clear vial from the back and studied it. "Passion fruit?" She shrugged, sprinkled it in the water, considered it briefly, and upended the vial.

An advantage of starting a new business in a new city had been its usefulness as a time filler, much as school, post-graduate work, and other jobs had been. But while those distractions had worked during the day, nights left her longing for dawn and the chance to lose herself in busyness again. She had hoped a new city, a seismic change in her career path would fill that empty space the intervening years hadn't. That is she had hoped that until she had looked up to meet Tom's eyes and the oxygen had evaporated from the room.

Since then, no amount of activity had been enough to make up for nights haunted by thoughts of someone's mouth, someone's hands, someone's body. Wondering...

Get real, girl. She put the container back on the shelf. If Tom was between girlfriends, it was surely only temporary. She drew a breath. After this silly awards banquet, they'd both be free.

Back to reality. She turned on the oven to warm the buns and muffins. Soon, the fragrance of brown sugar, vanilla, and passion fruit would perfume the shop.

Magdalena was freshening David's cup when she returned to the front.

"So what are you trying now?" she asked.

"Monkey orchid oolong."

"It was part of the shipment David sent us from Formosa a couple months ago," Magdalena said.

It seemed her partner had caught on to the fact she was there.

"Ahh, excellent." David took another sip. "Wonderful place, Formosa. Quite a varied geography for a small island. Amazing variety of tea grows on the cliffs there. One finds the best in the Fujian province, but, of course, the local demand is tremendous. Not easy to get the growers to part with their harvest for export. And you've enhanced it with allspice."

"All Magdalena's doing." She took a seat at the counter beside their tea scout. Even sitting, she had to tilt her head back to talk to David. "She's the one with the gifted taste buds."

"Well, it certainly shows."

Was her friend blushing? After a career as a Las Vegas showgirl, she hadn't thought there was much left that could embarrass Magdalena.

"So did you fill David in on our problem?"

Magdalena looked lost.

"You know, with the Celestial Harmony blend."

"Oh, yes. David, remember, I told you about what happened with the guests at the Imperial Hotel after they tried the samples we'd left for them."

"Right. What a story! I wish the tea could claim credit, but apparently, other than its well-known relaxing benefits, I think the most likely causes were simply being in Las Vegas, on vacation and in the company of an attractive partner."

He shook his head and took a deep sip of his tea as Magdalena propped her head on a hand and smiled at him.

****

Tom paused in the doorway of his outer office and waited until Candace finished her conversation, laid down her headset, and looked up at him.

"How's it going?" he asked.

It seemed that since he'd left the previous evening, a new collection of houseplants had been added to his secretary's workspace. Candace appeared cheerfully undeterred in her quest to add a touch of nature to the office despite the inevitable, silent demise of their predecessors. He was fairly confident that somewhere in her desk was a new sample of plant food she felt sure would counteract the office's artificial light and ventilation.

"Fine. That was the design team from the architect's office calling to re-confirm the meeting on Monday. They've finished the re-design on the West End project and are ready to present it."

"Good. I was wondering how they'd incorporate the new features Jim's interested in."

"It didn't sound like there was any problem."

"Okay, would you let Mr. McMasters know? I'm sure he'll want to sit in on it."

His secretary nodded and reached for her headset again as he pushed through the door into his private office. After a year, he was just beginning to get used to the Thomas Marco, General Manager sign on the door.

The new theater area was another extension of the original Outpost property, an addition that entailed additional expense. The concept of modeling their dinner show area/concert venue on one of London's West End theaters had been Gentleman Jim's. And as with most things when done properly, it came with a hefty price tag.

When work was completed in the spring, they'd be able to bring in the kind of big-name entertainment that properties on the Strip did. The buzz such headliners generated would add cachet to their name and eventually, they'd recoup their investment. Eventually. Just had to keep their ship afloat 'til then.

He picked up the messages in his inbox, opened his desk drawer, and found his reading glasses. He didn't like using them unless he had to, but reading Candace's dainty script was beyond him. Was it male pride that kept them concealed in a desk drawer? He resisted acknowledging being anything less than one hundred percent. Being physically fit had been a priority stretching back to his need to stay out of the reach of some of Mom's boyfriends.

Later, defending himself in a few of the foster care situations he'd found himself in had been easier. By that time, his build plus a certain look in his eye had been sufficient to back most bullies down. His last patrol in Afghanistan had left its mark, but minor problems with vision as well as setting off metal detectors when he went through airport security were small inconveniences compared with what so many others had left half a world away from their fellow Americans.

He scanned the first message.

Steve Carrillo from personnel on expanding the hours of operation for the pool and cabana area; he needed to get together to discuss estimates of projected new hires and budget. Fortunately, for the bottom line, most of the job openings would be minimum wage. It wasn't fun being a penny pincher, but that was the long and short of it.

Message from food services—their seafood supplier in Tacoma had notified them that projections of this year's salmon run were down and consequently prices were expected to rise.

He inhaled sharply as he read the final one. Edmund Chancellor had called from the U. K., Candace had written, with a question about the quarterly report. Would it be possible to send it via e-mail instead of trusting it to the post this time? Thank you ever so much.

Edmund Chancellor was one of Gentleman Jim's principle British investors. First Elspeth Porter-Hayes, now Chancellor. The buzzer on the intercom beeped as he shook his head.

"Yes, Candace."

"Tom, Sandy Korman from the auditing firm in Henderson is on the line. She wanted to let you know they've received notice from the lender holding the note on the West End construction project asking for the latest quarterly fiscal statement before they renew the loan. Shall I put her through?"

"Sure." He took a deep breath and picked up his phone. Was it living in a desert climate that made him picture huge birds circling lazily overhead, eyeing the Imperial speculatively?

****

Finishing up in the kitchen, she joined Magdalena and David in the pantry. Magdalena was holding an open canister for their tea scout. David opened his eyes to look her way with a smile.

"Magdalena tells me this is your winter blend. Currants, cloves, orange peel, cinnamon, and vanilla along with something tart." He studied it.

"Cranberries," her partner supplied. "We spotlighted this tea in our holiday gift baskets last year."

"We gave out samples of it during the Christmas season to put shoppers in the mood even if December in Nevada isn't the stereotypical winter scene."

"I can understand. Speaking of holiday gifts, have you two ever thought of offering tea sets and the like? Some of my clients sell whole tea services, cream and sugar duos, mugs with lids that double as coasters."

"We have our travel mugs, but that's been it." Magdalena turned to her.

"Those are popular with the locals. We offer a discount on refills. Of course, a lot of our business is one-time, people here on vacation."

"Well, I can forward information to you, if it's something you might want to pursue. The chap and his wife I visited in Monterrey call their line sip ware. And what is this?" He opened another canister and took a breath. "Oh, yes, chai. Unparalleled when steamed with warm milk and honey."

Could the man live on tea? With his negative body-mass index, it didn't seem out of the question.

"And I see you're incorporating some Native American products." David ran his finger down a line of jars. "Blackberry leaves, orange bergamot, lemon verbena. Sometime next year, I want to get back into the rainforests of India and Ceylon. See what the native peoples are using. One can learn so much that way. I've tasted some wonderful cardamom from there, gingery with a pinch of fire."

Magdalena made a soft sound like a moan.

"I'll make a note to send some your way. Ah, chamomile. Excellent. Nothing better for insuring a good night's sleep."

"Usually not a problem for us after a full day on our feet."

Magdalena's fingers seemed to linger on David's as he handed her the chamomile.

"Jasmine, yes. And silver tips, lovely, peachy character those. Tickles the palate, doesn't it?" David seemed to be talking to himself as he surveyed the shelves, his acolyte Magdalena trailing in his wake.

Cinna was turning to go when David stopped abruptly and tapped a glass container with a forefinger.

"Organic rooibos, yes. Use this much?"

"Occasionally someone will ask for it." Magdalena looked up at him. "And it makes a good caffeine-free herbal blend with other teas."

He turned to them both, wrinkling his brow.

"Just mulling something over. I've heard it used… Yes, I'm sure I have. I've heard that some Asian herbalists use it in combination with ashwagandha root and a bark. Can't quite place which one now." He tapped the container with his fingers before shaking his head. "It'll come back. Anyway, as I recall, it's a folk medicine to enhance the midnight hours, shall we say."

Wonderful. She looked at Magdalena gazing up at her tea guru.

Why didn't this stuff come with warning labels?

Chapter Eight

Tom checked the time on the dashboard as he headed west down Route 159. Behind him, the sun was already over the horizon. Getting ready for the day had entailed a detour over to the Imperial to collect the climbing gear from his old room where he'd dumped it after his last climb. He'd waved to Elspeth Porter-Hayes and her companion breakfasting in the Cork and Cleaver where he'd grabbed a double espresso to go.

It'd been a while. His last climb had been B.C.— Before Cinna. The weeks since finding her again had been split between his work at Imperial and drinking more tea than he could have imagined. All while doing his best to insinuate himself into her life. He lowered a window and adjusted the mirror.

The asphalt rolled smoothly under his tires. His SUV might be no comparison to the Jag, but on a venture like this, it couldn't be beat. Even with the odometer set to turn over.

Once an ancient seabed, the oxidized red and orange remnants he traveled through were usually enough to command his interest. Today with other things on his mind, he barely noticed them.

The unexplained cash drain at the Imperial continued. He drummed a hand on the steering wheel. He'd had the business office run the interim numbers before he'd left the night before, a clear loss of several thousand dollars already this month. In the larger scheme of millions of dollars flowing in and out of Vegas, it was a drop in the ocean, but it was a loss he couldn't explain. It was keeping them on the red side of the balance sheet and investors didn't care for questions that couldn't be answered.

He bit his lip and willed himself to relax. This excursion was all about working off some of the tension he was feeling in his back and shoulders before the awards banquet and the chance at winning industry recognition for their hard work. Besides boosting their marketability, winning would surely impress his girl. *His girl?*

He had to be making progress there, didn't he? The slight intake of breath when he casually moved a fraction too close, the start when his hand brushed hers, the catch in her voice and the way her long lashes trembled when she looked up at him had to be good signs. And last Monday morning when he arrived at the shop in his new suit, her smoky blue eyes had lingered an instant too long on the way it showcased his shoulders, before looking away as if guilty.

Down, boy. He loosened his grip on the steering wheel letting his speed slow as the Red Rock Canyon National Conservation Area sign came into view. Fifteen miles west of Las Vegas, the sandstone peaks and rock formations could be seen from the Strip.

Tonight was just another step in his campaign to win her. Fortunately, she lived with a roommate so he could avoid any temptation to rush things when he brought her home. And if the Imperial took the award for best small independent hotel-casino, another date would be in order to celebrate.

He pulled in back of a Humvee, the driver leaning out to talk to the Bureau of Land Management ranger. Maybe he could arrange a quiet table at the Reserve and show her the Imperial's fine dining, followed by an after dinner drink at Keys, their piano bar, and a little slow dancing, her body curving into his, his hand on her lower back. If the signals looked promising, his room was still available at the Imperial. If not, well, it wouldn't be his first cold shower.

The driver of the Humvee had finished his conversation and was pulling away. He shifted gears and moved up to where the ranger was standing patiently, clipboard in hand. Outside the ranger station, two wild burros tugged at clumps of weeds beside a twisted Joshua tree.

He lowered his window.

"Hello."

"Good morning, sir. Welcome back."

"Thanks. It's been a while." He took the clipboard, signed his name and the time, and showed his identification.

"Thank you, Mr. Marco. I see you'll be heading over to the Calico Hills area."

"Right. I've got my climbing gear packed. Many visitors today?"

"I've checked in two female climbers so far. You should have a straight shot. How's your water situation?"

"I've got some to drink before I start and more to take with me." He nodded at the cooler beside him.

"Sounds good. Well, enjoy your day, sir."

"Thanks." He raised his hand and let the car roll forward onto the loop road that circled the preserve.

He'd discovered the popular nature reserve on the Mojave's eastern edge shortly after arriving in Vegas. Ten years of army conditioning had left him with no desire to go soft. And demanding physical exercise had helped keep his mind off other things.

Like his missed chance with the slip of girl who'd set his pulse racing years ago, like no one before or since.

The series of colored cliffs dubbed the Calico Hills lay just a mile past the visitors' center. A favorite for local rock climbers, he was lucky he wasn't standing in line behind other weekend athletes taking a break from Vegas's better-known attractions.

He coasted off the road into the pullout and parked. He popped the trunk and found a bottle of water in the cooler. He took his time with it, letting the water in his mouth warm to body temperature before swallowing.

The sun was high enough now to display how the cliff's red Aztec sandstone contrasted against the frosted gold limestone below it. Strata descended in rippling bands of pinks, yellows, and purples downward to where stunted aspens and bristlecone pines clung to a borderline existence among cliff debris.

On the cliff face, he watched a climber make her way upward. At the base, another climber looked over to wave at him as he got out. He waved back, glancing up, his senses tingling as a shadow passed overhead. A golden eagle? He shaded his eyes to watch it sweep in a wide circle. Objects in the distance shimmered as waves of heat rose from the desert floor.

Centuries before the area had been a lush grassland. Once he'd hiked the Sandstone Quarries trail to see the Indian petroglyphs in Brownstone Canyon that depicted an ancient hunt for Bighorn sheep when rain had been more plentiful. Nowadays, the dry desert vegetation managed to support scavenging populations of gray fox and coyotes along with scorpions, Gila monsters, and several kinds of rattlesnakes.

He collected his gear from the trunk, added two bottles of water to his utility belt, and pulled on his fingerless climbing gloves. Cinching the neck strap to his helmet, he closed the trunk.

The second female climber had begun her assent. Both women were tackling one of the higher sections where the cliffs topped out at over two thousand feet. Needing to be back in town by early afternoon, he had already decided to try a shorter climb.

He hiked over the broken escarpment to the base of the section he'd selected and surveyed it. Not as high as other parts, it still offered challenges. About two-thirds of the way up, the limestone face sloped outward, then back inward just above forming a natural ledge. He wasn't real familiar with it and it'd require some careful maneuvering.

He uncapped one of the bottles, took a long slow drink, and wiped his forehead. Taking his time to finish most of the water, he plotted his way up. Putting the bottle back in his utility belt, he felt for the first handhold. Still morning, the rocks were reflecting the Nevada heat.

The first part shouldn't have been difficult, but it required more effort than he remembered. A month away from climbing showed. He concentrated on finding handholds and footholds as he inched upward. Nearing the ledge, he secured himself to the rock wall and finished his first water bottle. Sweat stuck the shirt to his back. He took the opportunity to wipe his face and neck.

He looked up, analyzing what lay ahead. The easiest course up had brought him to six feet below the outcropping. Now he'd have to start moving laterally, stopping to secure his rope before hauling himself around the remainder.

He moved up sideways, secured his line over a protruding rock, and tested it. His fingers and nails were showing the effects of the climb. Maybe when he got back to the Imperial he ought to swing by the spa. Skin like sandpaper sure wasn't going to get him anywhere with—

Hell! He gasped, holding his breath as the rope above him suddenly frayed and sent him lurching awkwardly. He had seconds to decide—swing for the ledge or belly slide down the jagged cliff face.

His feet caught the edge, one slipping off as he propelled himself forward sprawling onto the ledge, hands scrambling for something, anything to hold onto.

Most of his body was off the slanted outcropping. Limestone. How long would it hold two hundred plus pounds before crumbling? Would moving make it better or worse? He hadn't seen anyone else since he'd started his climb. Were the two female climbers finished and gone? Would anyone hear him if he yelled?

The arid silence swallowed up his cry.

"C'mon, Marco, remember your Ranger training— think, assess the situation, maximize your resources." He shut his eyes and counted his heartbeats until they slowed.

Slowly, he reeled in his fraying rope. It caught

momentarily before the final fibers snapped where it had separated. He didn't have much. He couldn't finish scaling the rest of the cliff or dare working his way down without a rope. The damaged shards of his cell phone prodded his groin. Not that he'd be able to get reception out here anyway. He undid his belt and edged the empty water bottle out, careful to limit his motions. With the downward tilt of the ledge, a wrong move could send him rolling out of control. Tying the end of the belt around the bottleneck, he secured the other end to the frayed fibers of the rope. Plastic would glitter in the bright sunlight. He lowered the rope over the crumbling rock edge and let it swing. Movement and noise were what attracted attention in the wild. A shadow passed over him. Hopefully, it wasn't a buzzard scouting out his next meal.

Time was slipping away. At sundown, the park closed. Then someone at the ranger station would realize he hadn't signed out, come looking for him, and find his car. But, by then, he'd have missed picking up Cinna for the banquet. No use to dwell on that now. The rough limestone was doing a number on his face. A drop of sweat made its way down his cheek. He captured it with his tongue, the saltiness actually tasting good. It was clear dehydration was setting in. There was still the second bottle of water. If he paced himself, he could make it through the heat of the afternoon. Surely, the Park Service would find him before the evening chill caught him exposed on the rock.

Swing, sway. *C'mon, someone, notice*. He let the rope play out.

The pain in his chest was real and getting worse. He took shallow breaths. Hopefully, he hadn't collapsed a lung. He swung the belt against the rocks and glanced at his watch. Maybe he could take a sip now. The sun, overhead in a cloudless sky, was blazing down. Had he stopped sweating? Not a good sign.

He edged the remaining bottle toward him, tucking it against his shoulder and working off the cap with his free hand. His hands were rough now, his fingers growing numb. The cap didn't want to move. His throat hurt to swallow. He gave a quick twist.

Shit! The bottle slid away from him, rolling to the edge. He made a final grab for it, speechless with pain. His fingers grazed it as it caught on the edge and cartwheeled off. Droplets of water were thrown up mockingly, spiraling into the air. He shoved his bleeding hand against the limestone to keep his momentum from following it.

Relax, relax. He put his head down and closed his eyes. *Concentrate on just breathing*. He found himself slipping in and out of consciousness, losing track of things. Where was he? Somewhere hot, dry…Afghanistan?

Just breathe. Breathe. Slow and steady, Dougherty. Don't force it. We've all got to ride this out. Wait on help. You know they'll be coming. We take care of our own. Come on, kid. Hang in there, buddy. The helicopters should be almost here. Think about home, going home. Think about the green hills back home. The rescue helicopter…

There was noise somewhere. He shook himself. Not a helicopter. It had come in time for him, for the rest of them, but not for Dougherty. His platoon would be rotated stateside, but Dougherty would return home to the green hills of West Virginia another way.

Somewhere below there was noise and a shout. He shook his head. He had thought his flashbacks and nightmares had ended once he'd gotten out of Walter Reed and made a new life in a new place.

"Marco, Marco, is that you?"

He gritted his teeth against the pain and drew a shallow breath, the effort filling his lungs with flame.

"Marco! Marco?"

"Polo!" he screamed once before he fainted.

Chapter Nine

Magdalena stood against the bedroom door, bracing it with her back, her dark eyes widening.

"Well?"

Her roommate held up a finger and waited an instant before she spoke.

"Cinna, the only way that man could look better in that tuxedo is if he were taking it off."

"What happened to David? I thought he was the one who was setting your heart aflutter."

"Just because I'm smitten doesn't mean I'm blind, girl," her roommate said.

Cinna put the comb down and smoothed the fall of the gold lamé dress over her hips. "The more I fool with my hair the more curls I end up with. So what do you think?" She turned to face her friend.

"The pair of you are going to stop traffic. Those honey-butter highlights we added to your hair are just the finishing touch. Here." She handed her the clutch purse from the dresser. "You may not consider the two of you a couple, but everyone at the convention center will."

She started to reply, but Magdalena interrupted her as she reached for the doorknob.

"Yeah, yeah, I know. Not a couple, not dating, not interested, right!"

She caught her breath as Magdalena held the door

for her and Tom turned to greet her. She stopped dead in the doorway buying a minute to compose herself as she fiddled with her skirt.

The midnight-black tux hung on him like it had been custom-tailored. Maybe it had been. As manager of one of the newest and hottest properties in Vegas, he probably had any number of social black-tie events to attend. And she was wearing a dress from a secondhand shop. She automatically extended her hand as he held out his.

He tilted his head, regarding her as he drew her toward him, a smile deepening at the corner of his mouth. The green glint in his eyes that had once haunted her dreams was back.

"You look wonderful."

"So do you." She flushed and bit her lip. "I mean…"

"Yeah, it's a little like prom, isn't it?"

"I wish I had a camera to take a picture of you two kids." Magdalena leaned against the doorframe grinning. "But the photographers at the banquet should love you."

Damn, it wasn't fair how the tuxedo accentuated the dark line of his brows and lashes, the intensity of his eyes. The sun-brown of his hair seemed infused with gold tonight while the strong planes of his face, even the crook of his nose made an interesting juxtaposition against the simple elegance of his tux. She needed to get out of the apartment. Maybe on the street she could grab a breath of fresh air.

Oh, no, he was watching as she fanned herself with a hand.

"So what are your plans for tonight?"

Tom broke off his gaze to look over at Magdalena who was regarding them with a mischievous grin.

"The ugly stepsister? No ball for yours truly. I'm going back to the shop to help close. My friend from the Silver Strike is pinch-hitting for us along with David Witheroe."

"Your tea scout? So he made it to town."

"Last night. He was nice enough to offer to stay with Barbara this afternoon. After we close, I may take him out and show him some of the local sights to thank him."

"Wait a minute." Tom reached into his suit coat and took out his wallet. Extracting a business card, he found a pen. "Here, why don't you take him to dinner at the Imperial? My treat for all you've done for Cinna and me." He wrote a few words on the card and handed it to Magdalena. "Give this to the maître d' at the Reserve and he'll find a table for you. It's got a view of the city that can't be beat."

"Thanks, Tom. Well, it looks like a good time for all tonight. I'll be crossing my fingers for you two." She winked at Cinna as she held the door for them.

"Don't hurry home!" Cinna heard her call as they started down the stairs.

In the car, she pushed her hair up off the nape of her neck to cool herself. The sweltering humidity wasn't helping. Her curls felt damp. She shook her hair out as Tom opened his door and took his time lowering himself into the XK, settling himself in and taking a deep breath.

"Are you all right?"

"Oh, fine. Thank God for air conditioning." He adjusted the controls on the dash.

It seemed she wasn't the only one feeling the heat.

He shifted gears and pulled out into the street. His hand on the gearshift was inches from where her dress fell away from her bare knee. Her skin still tingled from the heat of his hand on the small of her back as they descended the stairs, his fingers running down the inside of her elbow as he helped her into the car.

"I think I see lightning over there." He pointed in the distance. "We may be in for some weather later."

"Is this the right time of year? I haven't adjusted to life in the desert yet."

"The end of it. Most of Vegas's moisture comes in the spring."

"What brought you out here to live?" Talk to Tom, Magdalena had urged. Give the man a chance for heaven's sake. Find out what he's like now. People do change, you know.

"I had two tours of duty in Iraq, one in Afghanistan. The last one ended early, but I'd gotten used to a hot, dry climate."

"Mr. McMasters said you were wounded."

"Not as bad as a lot of the guys. Anyway, one winter in D.C. was enough to persuade me I wanted warmer temperatures when I got out."

"So Vegas?"

He shrugged. "It wasn't like I had a hometown to go back to. Des Moines was probably as much of one as any place I lived. After the service, I had the idea I could play cards while I looked around for something permanent. It didn't take long to figure out I wasn't as good as I thought I was. There's better money to be made working at a casino than playing in one for most of us."

He was quiet as he negotiated his way onto the highway.

"Have you been to the convention center, Cinnamon?"

She shook her head. "With Magdalena and I running the business ourselves there just isn't free time for much else. Even when the shop is closed, we're busy re-stocking, trying new varieties. I did get down to the Strip." She caught her breath. "I was at the Cote d'Azur the other day for lunch."

"It's a lot of work to get a business going."

"More than I was aware of when I moved out here. My parents, and I guess most everyone, thought it was pretty hair-brained. That's why the question about our Celestial Harmony blend threw us for a loop. We've put so much time and all the money we had between us into SpecialTeas, especially Mags. This whole thing has been her brainchild."

"I wouldn't worry about it, Cinna." His long, warm fingers found hers, caressing the inside of her wrist, her hand enveloped in his as it lay alongside her thigh.

Come on. This wasn't the kind of thing two non-dating people on their way to dinner did. She closed her eyes. How long had it been since a man had touched her? Did it show how much having someone just hold her hand affected her? And why was she suddenly conscious of the ivory, lace teddy underneath her finery that Magdalena insisted she buy?

Say something!

"So, so how did you meet Jim McMasters?" Her voice sounded husky.

"Oh." He laughed and actually moved his hand back to the steering wheel.

Great.

"I met him at a bar on the Strip where I was filling in for someone. Working part time was a good way to earn money and arrange my hours while I went to UNLV on the G.I. Bill. Jim was nursing a local beer, bemoaning the lack of a good lager, and we got talking. You've seen how friendly he is. He doesn't know a stranger. He'd come out here looking for an investment property. A realtor had taken him over to the Outpost Casino, which was up for sale, and he asked my opinion about it. About its viability for re-development, you know. I went with him for another look and we started brainstorming.

"He returned to the U.K. and I really didn't expect to hear from him again. But then he lined up a group of investors there and they made an offer for the Outpost. He asked me to work with him during the renovations. It took the better part of two years before we were ready to open. Construction isn't finished yet. We're still working on the new addition where we'll offer big name shows." He slowed to turn into the parking garage.

Across the street, the convention center was bright with lights, a sign welcoming the Las Vegas Hospitality Industry Association Dinner. At something over three million square feet, the complex was immense. Tom pulled up to the attendants' booth and handed his keys to a parking valet while a doorman opened her door for her.

She adjusted her neckline while he came around to offer his arm. It hadn't gotten any cooler. The air felt close.

"Ready?"

She took a breath and slid her arm through his as they crossed the pedestrian bridge to the Center. It sure was feeling like they were a couple, no matter how much she professed otherwise.

Inside the ballroom, the wait staff in black and white uniforms was circulating through the crowd with trays of canapés. Conversation and laughter drowned out whatever background music might have been playing.

"Can I get you something from the bar?" he asked.

"Sure, white wine, please."

She shook her head as a waiter approached with a tray. With her stomach in knots, she didn't need to challenge it with anything exotic.

The room was crowded with hundreds of people in fancy dresses and tuxedos, certainly more designer couture than she'd ever seen in one place. The sparkling lights of the chandeliers were answered by the winking jewels and sequined gowns below. Most of the movers and shakers of the city were sure to be in attendance. Some of the faces she recognized from media coverage. Probably all were Cristal drinkers instead of tea. Mercedes and Cadillacs had dominated the line of cars they'd waited in. She'd even spotted a Rolls Royce or two.

Tom was coming back, glass in hand, along with an older gentleman with an impressive head of white, wavy hair.

"Cinna." He handed her the wine glass. "This is Bill Rollins, a member of poker's Hall of Fame and a hospitality host at the Oasis Casino. Bill, this is a friend of mine, Cinnamon Smith."

"Just Bankroll, my dear." He bent over the hand

she gave him.

"Of course, probably everyone in Vegas has heard of you." Even holed up in a teashop, it was impossible to escape the advertising bearing his name and likeness—the Oasis Casino presents Bankroll Rollins in its Legends Lounge. Come join poker's living legend at the place where dreams become reality! Many of the town's highest rollers played at the Legends Casino.

"It's nice to meet you."

"And what do you do, little lady, besides making Tom here look good?"

As Bankroll pretended an interest in the tea trade, standing close enough to look down her dress, a steady stream of Tom's acquaintances came up. By the time the waiters and their trays had disappeared, she was half convinced her name was Cinnamon Smith SpecialTeas.

"I think…" Tom waved across the room at someone and took her elbow. "I think that's Dolores and Brielle from the Imperial over there. We all should be seated together."

The two women were waiting as Tom guided her through the crowd. The Imperial's assistant manager was standing with a slight auburn-haired girl.

"Cinna, I think you know Dolores."

"Yes." She offered her hand. "You took me to meet Mr. McMasters the other day."

"Right. It's nice to see you again," Tom's assistant manager said. "You look lovely."

"And this is Brielle Bennett, our assistant day shift supervisor."

Was there something familiar about the girl?

"Hi. I don't know if we've met, but maybe you've been in our shop? It's SpecialTeas. We're in the

Fremont Street Extension Mall," Cinna said.

The girl's large brown eyes behind oversized glass frames studied her.

"Could be. I'm in and around Fremont Street a lot," she said. "I like to get out and get some fresh air after a day at work and stretch my legs."

"So what do you think of all this?" Tom turned to face the crowd. "Quite a get together, isn't it?"

"It's great," Brielle said. "I've never seen so many big names in one place."

"You can't completely appreciate what all this means unless you know how much work it was getting to this night," Dolores raised her glass to Tom and turned to her.

"Probably the Outies more than anyone. Outies are what the employees who used to work at the Outpost are known as," Dolores explained. "Some of them returned after Jim McMasters bought it."

"Were there many who came back?"

"No. Most had moved on to new jobs by then. Some who did were curious to see what could be made of it, to be a part of its reincarnation. While the location was good, the Outpost had definitely seen its better days. And then the Imperial was lucky to pick up new employees like Brielle."

Her companion looked down at her drink and shook her head.

"She's pulled our chestnuts out of the fire on more than one occasion. The reason we're here tonight is due to our staff." Dolores laid a hand on Brielle's shoulder and looked up at Tom. "You know, you and Gentleman Jim presented an incredible vision of what we could hope to accomplish in that first senior staff meeting when you talked about working our way up to a five-star rating one day."

"Unfortunately, not everyone got the message." Tom shook his head.

Dolores smiled at the young woman beside her. "Brielle has."

"Oh, I'm glad for the experience. I feel like I've learned so much working at the Imperial. I don't mind pitching in to lend a hand when it's needed."

Tom had started to say something as an announcement interrupted them.

"Ladies and gentlemen, if I may have your attention. Please begin making your way to the ballroom where our association banquet is set to begin shortly."

She and Tom followed Dolores and Brielle into the next room where white-linen circular tables and covered chairs were set under crystal chandeliers. Waiters in dinner jackets were filling water goblets.

"We're up there, Tom." Dolores pointed to a table near the front.

A cloud of aftershave enveloped her as Tom pulled out a chair for her.

"Rollins, what are you doing here? I thought the people from the Oasis were over there?" Tom raised an eyebrow at the man sliding into the seat beside her.

"Oh, they are. We're not up for any of the awards this year. I traded my way around. Like the view better here." He winked at Marco.

She gave Bankroll a bright smile. After all, the Oasis might be in the market for tea too. Imperceptibly, she inched her seat closer to Tom's.

He turned his head to smile at her. "So do you need

a refill, Cinna?"

"Not now." She needed to keep her wits about her and deal with the fact that the slight fragrance of Tom's soap was more enticing than Bankroll's exotic cologne.

"How about you?"

He shook his head. "I made the decision years ago to pass on alcohol. With my family history, I couldn't believe it'd be a good choice."

The emcee at the podium was making some welcoming remarks as waiters entered carrying trays laden with sushi appetizers.

"So tell me about yourself, Cinnamon. What brought you to Vegas?" Bankroll popped a whole sashimi in his mouth.

Bankroll pretended an interest as she sketched out the route that had brought her to Vegas, her back toward Tom. She could overhear him talking about business with the others at the table. She must have been retreating as Bankroll leaned in toward her. Without breaking off his conversation, Tom casually draped his arm around the back of her chair.

"So how is everything?" His lips grazed her ear where an earring swayed as Bankroll turned to outline a past poker triumph to others at the table.

"It's wonderful." *Careful*. If she turned to look at him, their mouths would meet. He had to know it and he wasn't moving. "I'm not used to this kind of thing. I'm afraid the clock is going to strike twelve and I'm going to turn back into Cinna Smith in her SpecialTeas apron instead of a fancy dress."

"The apron's nice, too." He batted an earring with a finger and then slowly traced his way down her neck.

Come on now. What happened to just going to a

dinner together? Was he changing the rules? He must know how he looked in that tux and he was using it. *Remember the pre-Vegas version of Tom Marco you knew back in Des Moines* she reminded herself. The heartbreak he'd left behind him.

She scooted her lobster tail to the side of the dinner plate their waiter set down and started on the prime rib.

"No lobster? That's good eating, little lady." Bankroll Rollins frowned.

"Not for me. I don't eat shellfish. Do you want it?" she offered.

"Waste not, want not." He hoisted it off her plate and onto his own.

Tom gave her a wink.

She had finished her dinner when Dolores bent down over her shoulder.

"Cinna, Brielle and I are making a run to the restroom before dessert and the presentations. Do you want to come with us?"

"Sure, thanks." Tom got up to help with her chair.

"Dinner has been wonderful," she said as they maneuvered around the tables toward the door.

"Hasn't it? Although I think our chef at the Reserve could give them a run for their money. Have you eaten there, Brielle?"

Her co-worker shook her head. "No, by the time I'm finishing up, I'm usually just interested in getting back to my own place and crashing."

"You've put in some marathon days, but I guess you're only young once."

The ladies' lounge with its leather upholstered armchairs and recessed lighting was probably nicer than the facilities in most private homes. She was touching up her lipstick as Dolores combed the heavy swing of her salt and pepper hair at the mirror.

"I don't think I'm going to do much about this mop." Stray curls were escaping despite Magdalena's efforts. She found a comb and pushed her hair back stubbornly and re-secured the silver barrette.

"You look great. That dress was made for you," Dolores said.

"Thank you." She was trying to avoid the reflection in the mirror, gazing at the stranger in the clinging lamé dress, the dangling earrings, the tangle of highlighted ash-blonde hair. That person looked too much like someone who might actually date someone wearing a tuxedo. Where was the anonymous tea and crumpets server she was used to seeing?

"Well, it's almost time." Dolores checked her watch and turned to Brielle washing her hands at the sink. "We'll see what our hard work has done for us."

"Who else is nominated?" Cinna asked.

"The Desert Vista Inn and the Meridian in our category. They're real competition. Both have been in business for a lot longer than we have. The Meridian took home the award last year."

"Don't you think just the fact the Imperial has done so much in only a year is going to work in our favor?" Brielle dried her hands and checked her make-up.

"I do. We'll see if they agree with us. I know we couldn't be here today without staff members like you picking up the load for employees like Ron Caisson."

"I don't mind." Brielle closed her purse and looked over at Cinna. "Ron's our day shift supervisor. He's has had a rough couple years. It's been a lot to deal with." She looked embarrassed.

"We all know that, but sympathy only goes so far." Dolores got the door for them. "Tom already has enough on his shoulders. He's not on a rescue mission and Ron better get the message soon. Well, we need to get back in there so we can hold hands and think positive when our category comes up."

She didn't think she had room for dessert, but the waiters were serving baked Alaska topped with sparklers when they got back to their table. She managed a few bites while Tom played with his before pushing it away and signaling for coffee.

"Shouldn't be—" He paused as the lights in the ballroom flickered and conversation stopped.

"Sorry, folks." A man at the microphone adjusted the sound. "Some heavy weather is kicking up outside. A storm front is moving in. We're going to start now with the first presentation of the evening."

A number of winners had been announced and acceptance speeches given when the Imperial's category was called. She saw Dolores reach over to take Tom's hand as he enveloped hers in his.

"The Las Vegas Hospitality Industry Association annual award for best small independent hotel casino property this year is awarded to…"

"Come on. Come on." She heard Dolores whisper.

Tom's eyes were fixed on the podium, his posture rigid. She thought he was holding his breath. Her hand was crushed in his.

"The Imperial—Saint George's Consortium, Ltd., owners, James McMasters, chairman of the board, Thomas Marco, General Manager."

She heard screams from Dolores and Brielle as she was swept into a kiss. Eyes wide, she gasped for breath as Bankroll released her, stumbling back against her chair.

"Congratulations, little lady. Your man done himself proud."

Tom took Dolores's hand as they got up to move to the podium. Brielle moved over to sit beside her.

"Waiter!" Bankroll snapped his fingers at a passing waiter. "Let's have some of your bubbly over here. Fill 'em up!"

"Isn't this wonderful?" Brielle squeezed her arm. "Gentleman Jim is going to be over the moon. It's a shame that because of his age, he isn't up for late nights."

She leaned forward listening as waiters brought glasses and champagne for the table. At her elbow, Bankroll was urging the server to keep it coming.

Tom stepped forward to speak into the microphone, tilting it upward.

"I can't accept this award without thanking the staff of the Imperial, the men and women whose hard work over the past several years has brought us here tonight. Most especially, of course, James McMasters whose vision and spirit of adventure and daring led him from the Royal Air Force to his remarkable career in private industry and then to this city and the formation of his board of investors. In his name, my assistant manager, Dolores Rivera Ruiz, the staff of the Imperial, and I thank you all tonight."

A crowd of well-wishers engulfed Tom and Dolores offering congratulations. She watched Tom catch his breath as an attractive female embraced him. Bankroll was standing with his glass as they arrived.

"To the Imperial. A job well done!"

"Thank you." Tom raised his glass, inclined his head, and replaced it on the table. His lips brushed her cheek as he sat.

"Congratulations." Could he feel how flushed she was? She took a sip of her champagne. *Come on!* It was just a kiss on the cheek. Tom was smiling at her.

Dolores was digging into her purse. "I'm going to find somewhere quiet and call Leon. I don't care if the game is tied or in double overtime. What about Gentleman Jim, Tom? Do you want me to call or would you rather?"

"Go ahead." He waved a hand. "I'm sure he's waiting. Probably having a nightcap in the Exeter Club. The desk will find him for you."

Dolores tucked her purse under her arm as she got up to leave.

Tom relaxed back in his chair to listen to the next presentation. One hand was draped idly across the back of her chair, close to the folds of her dress, his long, tanned fingers touching the fabric.

Was she doing a bad imitation of Magdalena meeting David Witheroe for the first time? Hadn't his abrupt exit from Des Moines been enough to cure her of her schoolgirl fantasies? Was this what Ed had called their Venus week? Were she and Magdalena both sending out signals? People around her seemed to be applauding something. Automatically, she joined in.

She drew a breath and turned to look at him.

"I guess you can all relax now."

"Yeah, it's been a long day. A long, six weeks since the nominations were announced. Of course, we loved the recognition, but this guy…" he reached out to touch the statuette. It resembled a free-form rendering of a flame… "is the icing on the cake. Lovely icing."

His thumb touched the line of her spine as he contemplated the award.

Oh, hell. She drained the last of her champagne.

"Our last award of the evening is our Lifetime Achievement for Excellence in the hospitality industry to be presented to the individual whose contributions have promoted the Las Vegas travel industry. And then folks, we're going to ask you to leave as quickly and expeditiously as possible. The National Weather Service is issuing a flash flood warning for low-lying areas of the city. Some of you who live farther out, particularly north of here, may want to leave first."

"Brielle, why don't you see what it's doing outside?" Tom suggested.

Around them, people were rustling and beginning to collect their things. She tried to give her attention to what was going on at the podium.

Brielle was returning with Dolores as the last thank-you speech was given.

"Chief, the weather is really getting bad," Dolores said. "Leon was saying that some of the streets are being closed and power to our place was off for a while."

"The street looks like a swimming pool," Brielle added. "There's lightning and—" She stopped as the lights in the hall flickered.

"I believe you. Cinna, are you ready?"

She was already on her feet.

"I should be all right," Dolores said. "I'm south of here. I'll drop Brielle off on my way. Tom, if you're going to get back, you and Cinna need to leave right now. These desert storms can get dangerous."

Great. She'd never cared for storms anyway. Her champagne glass was empty. She reached over to take a sip from Tom's glass. Brielle looked alarmed. Maybe she felt the same way.

"Okay, let's go. Dolores, you've got your cell phone if you get in a dicey situation. Try to enjoy the rest of the weekend." Tom got the chair for her.

She almost didn't notice him putting his arm around her as they moved with the crowd toward the exits. The sense of unease was spreading. Even inside the thunder was deafening. She stopped with Tom in front of the entryway windows, staring as lightning arced across the sky.

Could he read the fear on her face? Tucking her hand under his arm, he guided her through the crowd and across the pedestrian bridge to the garage. Sheltering in a corner, she could see sheets of rain being pushed like waves across the asphalt surface.

"You stay here. I'm going to find the Jag. It may take a while."

"No." She pulled on his coat. "You'll drown out there. It's dangerous. Wait for a valet."

"Don't worry. I passed all my water safety tests back in basic. Although I wouldn't count on getting the deposit back on this tux tomorrow." He took off his coat and covered his head with it. "You stay here and watch for me. Three honks—short, long, short."

He was gone before she could protest.

What was it with men? Big macho guy.

The queue for valet service was turning into a competition. With people holding out fifties and hundreds, it looked like the parking lot attendants were guaranteed a lucrative evening. Bullets of rain ricocheted like machine gun fire on the slick surfaces of cars crawling toward the exit.

She jumped as two enormous bangs shook the building. Something somewhere close must have been hit. She swallowed hard. The storm seemed to have an angry, vicious quality. Maybe it was just because it was such a contrast to the usual dry, sunny weather she had grown used to.

Cinna clenched her jaw as a spider web of lightning illuminated the parking garage and an explosion of thunder shook the ground. Where was Tom? Had he found the car? Given the circumstances, maybe it was understandable she was wishing for the reassurance of his solid presence.

She was shaking. Come on now. *Get over it*, she told herself. Act like an adult. It's only a—She screamed along with the others around her as the lights of the convention center went out and the parking garage and surrounding business district plunged into darkness.

Coming from somewhere were three beeps from a horn and a flicker of headlights. Short, long, short? She couldn't tell. Anyway it sounded British. She put her purse and hands over her head and ran toward the sound. The rain was blowing sideways. She hurled herself in the open car door.

"Okay?" Tom's big hand wiped her face.

"Yeah, sure," she gasped. "You could drown just getting out here."

"I don't know which is better right now. Trying to get out and go home, or staying put until the weather subsides."

He reached over to turn the radio up just in time to

hear breaking news. "Vegas Emergency Services is reporting the substation at Route 206 is down and two substations north of the city are experiencing intermittent problems with power supply. Coming up, we'll update our list of street closings."

He took his time following the slow line of departing vehicles. Puddles sent sprays of water up the windows. At the exit, he pulled over to the curb, shifted into park, and stopped to listen to the radio announcer's list of street closures. Between flashes of lightning, she watched the other cars creep out onto the deserted street.

"I don't know about getting you back to your apartment, Cinna." Tom turned the sound down and looked at her, shaking his head. "It sounds like downtown is taking a beating. The girls going south should be all right, but the north end is getting hammered."

"Please don't risk anything that's not safe."

"Oh, Lord, honey, you're shivering." He reached over to cover her hands with his, rubbing her fingers and raising them to his mouth.

"I'm okay. This dress isn't the warmest thing around."

"Let's get some heat on." Releasing her hands, he adjusted the controls and cleared his throat. "You know, I'm afraid we may run into some urban flooding. My place isn't that far. I should be able to make it okay. I've got a bed and a couch and we can wait it out there. What do you think?"

"F-fine." She wrapped her arms around herself. The clock had struck twelve, and the ball was over.

Chapter Ten

"Okay, this is it." He flicked the lights on. "We've still got power here fortunately. The bathroom is through here."

He pushed the bedroom door open. "You can take a hot shower. Towels are in the closet and at least one robe liberated from the Imperial. Help yourself."

"Thanks." Convulsing with shivers, it was the most she could manage.

"You go on. I'll fix you something to drink."

In the kitchen, he filled a mug with water and put it in the microwave. Cinnamon disappeared into the other room. The downpour had left little to the imagination. It'd been better than a wet T-shirt contest. The rain-soaked dress had clung to her form—bust, legs, rear, her damp curls glittering with droplets.

He jerked as the beeper sounded, and winced. He removed the cup and added a tea bag. There were other things he had to concentrate on now. He dunked the tea bag and frowned.

At the emergency room where they'd transported him, the park ranger had delivered the standard lecture on the necessity of checking out his equipment before attempting a climb. He'd listened in silence, biting his tongue and conserving his strength.

He was no expert, but the tea looked the right color. He discarded the tea bag and took the cup into the bedroom. Putting it on the bedside table, he slipped his usual choice of reading material under the bed. The water in the bathroom continued to stream. It was funny how appealing that water sounded in contrast to the deluge outside. How tempting it would be to slip into a hot steamy shower with a warm, soft, naked girl.

Easy, Marco.

The situation outside was bad and getting worse. The last report on the car radio had repeated the warnings about a stationary low front over the city and severe danger of urban flooding. God knows what was going on at the Imperial. Phone service was down along with the cable.

He found dry sweats in his drawer and took them out to the living room. The tux looked like a lost cause. Would the men's store accept the storm of the century as a sufficient reason? Even his socks were a sodden mess. He peeled them off and replaced everything. At least, he could hang the tux up. He found hangers in the closet along with the gym shoes he'd worn that morning and the climbing equipment he'd dumped there in his hurry to change.

He didn't need to look at it again. He'd had plenty of time stranded on the cliff face that afternoon to examine the frayed rope. He hadn't explained to the park service officer that his training as an army ranger had instilled an obsessive need to check his equipment before and after every mission. He'd drilled it into every platoon he led. He had examined it before the climb that morning and it seemed fine. Except somehow the rope's interior strands had been cut where they couldn't be seen. As if, someone had managed to snip the interior strands and weaken it.

An attempt on his life? A bad practical joke? He found his briefcase and snapped the clasps. Coiling his rope, he placed it inside. The sound of water in the bathroom had stopped. Other things demanded his attention now.

****

She turned her head to the side. Her eyelids felt like they were glued down. And what was that awful taste in her mouth? Cinna rubbed a hand across her face, flopped over, and pulled the sheet up around her nude body.

Nude? She sat up, pulling the sheet up around her, head throbbing.

Where the…? Nothing was familiar—the double bed, the lamp and clock radio on the nightstand, the terrycloth robe discarded on the floor. Why was it so hard to think?

Groggy, she swung her legs over the side and reached for it. There was something familiar about it. Something about being enfolded in its comforting softness last night before…before what?

She remembered something about a protracted, hot shower. The door to the bathroom was still ajar.

Her fingers caught on the raised stitching. She turned the robe over to read the embossed crest, a lion and a unicorn above two words in script. She stared, shivering in spite of the sunlight filtering through the blinds. The Imperial.

"Tom Marco." She closed her eyes, covering her face as she fell backward onto the bed.

The awards dinner, the thunderstorm, the streets closed because of flooding. He'd sweet-talked her into coming back to his apartment. She'd struggled out of her sodden clothing, into the heat of the shower, almost falling asleep as she stood in its welcome warmth. Then she'd put on the robe hanging on a hook in the linen closet and come back to spend the night in his bed. Alone she had presumed.

And then? She couldn't think. What was that taste in her mouth? She sat up and focused on the china mug beside the bed. She picked it up and swirled the remaining liquid around. There was tea residue at the bottom.

The mug had been sitting on the nightstand when she'd emerged from the bathroom. There'd been something off about its flavor, different, but at least it'd been warm. She'd sipped it, savoring the heat, feeling the tension from the storm ease, relaxing as her eyelids drifted shut. There had been a noise. Like a door opening? And a scent. Something male?

Oh, Cinna. She pressed her hands over her face.

Her chest felt tight. Had he used the damned Celestial Harmony tea he'd told her he'd had removed from the Imperial's breakfast buffet?

His weight on the edge of the bed, his hands smoothing back her tangled hair, his kisses down her cheekbone to the side of her neck as his long fingers undid the ties of the robe, spreading it open.

Cinna. His breath warm in her ear.

Her hands had found their way up the hard muscles of his chest, caught in his hair as he moved down beside her. He'd smoothed her thighs apart, whispering in her ear as his hands and then his mouth found her breasts.

Oh, Cinna! He had possessed her, using her body as he thrust and she wiggled against him seeking relief from the hands torturing her breasts, his mouth on her nipples. She'd screamed until she collapsed panting; he held her until he was satisfied as well. Satiated, he'd let her roll away and stood perfect in the pale light, untangling the sheets rejoining her and pulling the covers around them.

How many times had he found his pleasure? The night was a confused memory of teasing desire, extended release, enduring his lovemaking until he triumphed again. Her teenage daydreams had been filled with fantasies of what it would be like to spend the night in his arms. Reality had proven different. Her trust was broken now just as Rosemary's had been. Only she should have been smarter after her sister's example.

Damn, damn bastard! She stumbled out of bed, pulling the robe around her, and threw open the living room door. The apartment was as empty as she had guessed it would be. He'd finished with her. Back in the bedroom, she grabbed the mug and hurled it against the wall, tears blurring her eyes.

Evidently, one Smith girl hadn't been enough for him.

****

She took a deep breath before she turned the lock. The cabdriver who had picked her up outside Marco's apartment had been more than eager to describe the flood's destruction.

"They're saying eight to ten inches in four hours. More north in the downtown. That's better than twice what Vegas gets in a year, you know. People was crazy last night. I'm telling you, I coulda made a fortune if I'd wanted. They was offering anything to get across town. I wasn't about to chance it though. No way. Don't take much in the way of running water to sweep cars away. Especially under the overpasses. Those things can be death traps. They got rescue crews out today looking for some people missing."

She was grateful he hadn't commented on her attire—the wreck of her lamé dress, open-toed shoes still squishing at every step, damp underwear clinging. But then after driving a cab in Vegas, he'd probably seen it all.

"So what are they saying about the Fremont Street area?" she'd asked.

"Lotta damage. Lotta damage. The city got hit bad there." He'd shaken his head in disbelief. "Power's still out in most of downtown. It's gonna be a real mess for days. I've been out here coming up on fifteen years and I never saw the like."

Back home, she tore off her ruined finery, stuffing it down in the trash, sick of the sight of it. The apartment was empty. Maybe Magdalena had already gone down to the shop to look things over. Her cell wasn't on either. David, along with Rosemary and her friend, were probably getting a wild impression of the desert city.

She had taken a shower, concentrating on scrubbing her hair and body, avoiding the thought of Tom's hands on her. She needed to focus on the future, the day ahead. There was work to do if she and Magdalena were to save their business.

Once clad in jeans, a T-shirt, and old shoes, she had opted to walk the dozen or so blocks to the shop. With the power still out, traffic signals wouldn't be working even if the streets were passable

Branches and debris blocked gutters gushing with

muddy water. Two men were hauling a couch out to the curb to join a sodden armchair, mattress, and bedding as she passed. Storekeepers had begun getting rid of ruined furniture and merchandise; uniform looks of disgust on their faces as they called back and forth to each other, comparing losses.

What would their damage be? Luckily, most of the expensive equipment they'd purchased like the roaster and the tea press were up off the floor along with the tea canisters in the back room. The consumables in the refrigerator and freezer would have to be discarded. The flooring? What was their responsibility and what was the landlord's?

Fremont Street had taken her breath away. It looked like the power was still off or the casinos too disheartened to turn on their neon. Even the oversized Vegas Vic and Vickie signs had looked depressed.

The sun, shining in a flawless blue sky, seemed to mock the devastation. The mountains of trash on the muddy sidewalks were already beginning to reek. How long would it take city services to get around and remove it all? And what about vermin getting into the refuge?

"Cinna, getting ready to take a look?"

Adam Hrang from Jailhouse Rock Jewelry next door paused in his open doorway.

"Yeah, I want to see what the damage is." She gave the door a shove and put the key back in her purse. She took a step back as the smell greeted her. "Or maybe I don't. Have you seen Magdalena around?"

"No, I haven't. Kim and I actually spent the night here. We were working on some remounts when it started to get bad. We tried bailing out with buckets, but we couldn't keep up. There wasn't anywhere to put the water. We spent the night on top of the counter. You can imagine how much rest we got." He shrugged his shoulders wearily.

"How's your place look?"

"It's a disaster. Although considering our inventory, at least our stuff isn't damaged by water. Jewelry won't spoil. The gal down at the handmade paper place really took a beating. Ben over at the leather shop was by a while ago. He opened the door, took one look inside, and left. He's got a big investment in exotic hides—snakeskin, lizard, ostrich. Don't know how much of that kind of stock can be salvaged." He made a face.

"For us, it's just going to take a lot of cleaning up. Kim is making a run, trying to find cleaning supplies before everything sells out. We need a truckload of disinfectant."

"Yeah, all that is going to be in short supply." She took a deep breath and shoved the door open. It caught on something.

"Let me know if we can help. Be careful. You might want to wear a mask and gloves. You know the sewers backed up," Adam warned.

She raised a hand and went on in, stopping in the entryway. It looked like the surge of water had swept potted plants, tables, and chairs back against the counter before scattering them. A dwarf palm that had seen better days blocked her way. She rolled it away with her foot. Vases, napkin holders, menu cards, display canisters? It was hard to identify what was under the slime.

She grimaced and picked her way back to the

counter. Mud on the floor pulled at her shoes. At least, she assumed it was mud. A dark line on the wall showed how high the water had risen.

She found paper towels on a back shelf and absently wiped the counter, looking around. Yesterday, the large front window had given passers-by a tempting view of the shop—its pristine walls, spotless counters, and gleaming glass display cases. The tables had been bright with nosegays. The comfy, padded love seat in the corner piled with cushions. A mixture of aromas, exotic and familiar, had welcomed customers as they'd entered. *Yesterday*.

A year ago, she and Magdalena had examined the property as a potential site for their business. The small collection of eclectic shops in the up and coming Fremont Street area had appealed to them. A performing arts center for the north end was in the plans for the near future. Now probably most the local businesses were in the same fix. Small, independent stores, they operated on the same shoestring budget they did.

The amount of cleaning needing to be done before they could reopen was staggering, Sanitation would be doubly important for a food business. There'd be a health department inspection to pass before they could re-open. She bit her lip. Would the water have caused warping? The polished hardwood floor had been a source of pride. The chairs were metal with padded seats. Scroll-back, they were reminiscent of an earlier era. They'd need to make contact with their landlord, but as a commercial renter of retail space, he was sure to be overwhelmed now.

Some of the cleaning they could do themselves, but

the city health inspectors would probably require the rest to be professionally sanitized before they would permit them to reopen.

Adam had said the sewers had backed up. She was putting off even looking in the restrooms.

No, she'd start at the kitchen area and the storerooms first. She stopped, gritted her teeth, and pushed through the louvered door into the back.

The pantry shelves were undisturbed. She ran her hand down the row of tin canisters—Pomegranate green tea, acerola from the Caribbean, ginseng and chamomile, the rare spring harvest oolong David had sent them from Taiwan, along with the South African rooibos and others. At least some of their pricy stock wouldn't have to be replaced when they finally got back to having customers. Small comfort since they wouldn't have any customers to worry about for a while.

She was using a trash bag and rubber gloves to empty the refrigerator when she heard noise in the front.

"Cinna? Cinnamon, are you here?"

What? It sounded like…

She dropped her trash bag and went out to the front, removing her gloves.

"Rosemary?"

Her sister, looking as pulled together as always, trim in designer jeans, T-shirt, and sweater knotted around her shoulders was looking around the front.

"Oh, Sis. I'm so sorry. This is heartbreaking. Ed and I were at the hotel when the skies opened last night. We decided to come down today and see what the story was. Things are at sixes and sevens with the convention. The Cote d'Azur has power, but, of course, not everyone is staying there."

Rosemary's friend, Ed, stepped up beside her, laying a hand on her shoulder as her sister looked at him. "The weather service called it a hundred years' storm and it looks like that's about right."

"I hate for you to see the shop this way. It used to look a lot better. Something we were proud of." Cinna waved a limp hand.

"I know, Sis. Mom and Dad were really impressed when they were out here and you've been remodeling too."

Hm, not really.

"Well, that was then. Right now I'm just taking a look at the situation. I don't know where Magdalena is. I hope she didn't get stranded somewhere. I was sorting through things in the back and throwing most of it away. That's where our kitchen and pantries are."

"It looks like the storm surge came up about three feet." Ed paused as the lights flickered on briefly before going out again.

"Maybe they're making progress. Once you get your power back and the fans going, things will start to dry out in this desert heat."

"If you have some more rubber gloves, we can help you, Cinna," her sister offered.

"No, really. I don't know how much I'm going to do today. Just more or less putter around. You didn't come to Vegas to deal with this mess."

"Oh, this could be our chance to be part of a once-in-a-lifetime occurrence. Right, Rosie?" Ed moved over to straighten a chair as the door behind him opened.

Rosemary had turned to answer him as the hanging

temple bells sounded.

"Tom? Tom Marco," her sister asked.

As if her day couldn't get any better.

Chapter Eleven

They were staring at each other, stock-still. In jeans and an old sweatshirt, Tom probably didn't look all that different from the college kid her sister had known back in Iowa.

"Rosemary?"

"Yes, wow!" She moved to offer her hand, smiling. "It's been a long time."

"I didn't realize you were in Vegas." Tom shook his head.

"We've been here a couple days. Just in time for the big flood. Ed, this is a friend of mine from college, Tom Marco."

A friend?

"Tom, I'd like you to meet Ed Dwyer. Ed has a medical practice in Chicago where I'm living now. We're out here for a convention at the Cote d'Azur on developing and promoting medical-related websites. We came up this morning to check on Cinna and see how she was."

"Glad to meet you." Ed shook hands with Tom. "Quite a city you have here. Bit different from Chicago."

"Usually. You aren't quite seeing it at its best. It'll bounce back quickly though."

"So what are you doing now? Do you live here in Vegas, Tom?" Rosemary asked.

"Yes, I do. I'm manager at the Imperial Hotel Casino, just a couple blocks over on Ogden. I moved out here after I left the army." He was still staring at Rosemary, hands on hips.

Like most men. Nothing really changed.

"Yeah, I heard you had enlisted."

Chat, chat, chat. Just like old home week. She shifted uncomfortably.

She must have attracted his notice. Tom tore his gaze away from Rosemary to look around.

"Looks like you took a hit too, Cinna. We've got power at the hotel. We managed to jerry-rig a generator to get basic services going. Some of our guests aren't up to climbing stairs. How are you doing on cleaning? I can cut a couple people loose from the Imperial to give you a hand."

"No!"

Rosemary turned to frown at her.

"Really, it's no trouble. We've pretty much got our situation under—"

"No, no. Just. Forget it." Her voice sounded shrill. Ed was looking at her too, his brow wrinkled. She had to get hold of herself before the whole sordid story spilled out to an audience. "I don't need anything. I'm just sorting through things now. Mags, Mags will help when she gets in." She shut her eyes and bit her trembling lip. The sight of him was too much to bear.

"She's probably still at the Imperial. She and David stayed over last night," Tom said slowly.

Of course. She'd forgotten the complementary dinner he'd offered them. It had probably been part of his scheme…to have her roommate out of the way when he brought her home. It seemed a lifetime ago now.

"David helped get things up and running last night. It was great having him there."

Nice someone had been on hand.

"Well…if you don't need anything." He paused searching her face. "I guess I'll go on back. Good seeing you again, Rosemary."

"Sure, Tom." Rosemary looked at her friend. "Ed, why don't you go on with Tom? You can see this end of town and take a look at the damage. We'll both have some stories to tell when we get back home. I'll help Cinna out here."

"Sure, if you don't need me."

"Come on. I'll show you the Imperial, the post-flood version anyway. We've been open just over a year." Tom held the door for Ed as the two men left.

"Tom Marco." Rosemary shook her head. "Small world. I always wondered what happened to him."

Cinna stared at her in disbelief.

"You came down on him pretty hard. What's going on, Cinnamon? He made a special trip over here when he's probably hip deep in mud and crud back at his hotel. Are you two dating?"

"Are you nuts? Never."

"What's wrong with Tom? He was a nice guy."

"Rosemary, get real." She couldn't keep it together anymore. She was hanging by a thread. Her night in Tom's bed, the flood, the shaky future of their fledgling business, the Celestial Harmony fiasco, Magdalena off somewhere with their tea scout.

"He's horrible. That piece of trash loser! He left you up the river. He takes ad-ad-advantage of…" Hot tears exploded as she doubled over, covering her face and trying to regain control. She felt nauseated.

"Tom Marco? He was always…" Rosemary put her arms around her and guided her to a chair. Flinching, she unknotted her sweater, put it on the dirty seat, and made Cinna sit down.

"Sis, did you think he was the father of my baby? That he was the one who got me pregnant?"

Cinna straightened, fighting to regain composure. Rosemary tore a paper towel off the roller and gave it to her.

"Is that it? Is that why you're acting so weird about him?"

"Well." Cinna wiped her face and steadied her trembling chin. "He, he was the one you were dating, wasn't he? I mean…"

Rosemary was shaking her head. "He wasn't the one who got me pregnant. Don't blame him. Oh, I had fallen for him. Any girl with a pulse would have. And he was such a nice guy. Hanging out at our house, helping Dad with those little fix-it projects he always had going, running Sage around, asking you to go places with us, eating Mom's home-cooked meals. I should have tumbled to it earlier that it was my family he'd fallen for, not me."

"What do you mean?"

"You know he grew up in foster care. His nose is the way it is because one of his mom's boyfriends got impatient with him and hit him with a beer bottle. Cinna, he was four years old. He just loved being part of a family. That was his attraction to me."

Rosemary righted another chair and covered the seat with paper towels.

"Oh, I had a major crush on him. And I was ready

to do the deed with him." Her face softened and she laughed ruefully. "We never quite got to it though. At a critical moment, he started babbling about our family."

"Our family?"

"Well, you actually. Something about that guy you ran cross-country with. How he didn't think he was trustworthy. Not exactly the kind of thing to put a girl in the mood. I told him off and stomped away."

"So you two never?"

"Never ever."

"So…?"

"Who knocked me up?" Her sister sighed. "Blame my vanity. You remember Rob Richardson?"

Rob Richardson. The name was familiar. Rosemary watched as she wrinkled her brow trying to think.

Rob Richard…

"*Mr*. Richardson!"

Her sister winced.

"Mr. Richardson? Rosemary, he was our art teacher. And he was like thirty."

"And married. As well as having that awful overbite. Yeah, it's disgusting. I was hurting over Tom. Rob used to come into that restaurant where I was working. Staying late over a cup of coffee, talking to me about my plans after college like he really cared. One night he asked if he could drive me home. Said he and his wife had separated." She rolled her eyes. "Turned out she was off in St. Louis taking care of her mother after she'd been injured in an accident. I guess my ego needed to believe I could attract someone."

"Oh, Rosemary."

"It was just a time or two, parked in his car behind

141

the football stadium. Maybe the fact I'd been a cheerleader did something for him. Anyway, it made me grow up fast. Mom and Dad turned out to be a lot smarter than I'd given them credit for. They told me I could use the pregnancy as an excuse for the rest of my life or as a turning point to make something out of it. So I got serious. I made the decision to give my baby and me the kind of lives we both deserved. I went to Iowa City to stay with Aunt Louise until the baby came, went through with the adoption, finished college, and made a career for myself."

"I'm sorry."

"I don't know if I am." Rosemary shook her head. "I mean somewhere there's a kid growing up with the family who loves him. He will turn thirteen this summer, hopefully with my drive, and let's be honest, my looks, and, I guess, his father's artistic talent. I've got the life I've worked hard for and maybe Ed." She smiled. "He's a good person, Cinna. I want you to get to know him. He and his ex co-parent their daughter. He knows all about my pregnancy and he's fine with the choices I made."

"I'm sorry you had to go through that."

"Well, it brought me where I am today, so I don't really mind it. I'm just sorry I wasn't more open with you. Tom didn't love me and leave me. With his background, he couldn't ever desert a child. I always wondered what had happened to him. When I got back from Iowa City, I tried to find him, but he'd dropped out of school. His uncle said he'd joined the army."

Cinna drew a shaky breath, crumbling the paper towel in her hand.

"Come on, if you'll show me where you keep the

rubber gloves, we can get busy cleaning up this mess, but Sis…"

She raised her head to look at Rosemary who was evaluating her critically.

"I hear a lot of emotion about someone you call a waste of time. You know…if you're not dating him, maybe you should."

****

"Boss!"

Tom looked up from across the atrium where Brielle was holding the door while Ron helped maintenance workers lug the rugs out of Memories, the hotel's gift shop. Dolores waved a hand at him as she picked her way across the muddy floor.

"How's everything? Didn't know if you'd make it in. Looks like you're ready to work," he said. His assistant manager had skipped her usual business attire in favor of a UNLV sweat suit that had seen better days.

"Oh, yeah. Streets are open now. It looks like you've got a good crew in here. Leon is parking the car. He's going to lend a hand. His office is closed since it's Sunday. No damage there, but no power either."

"Good. It's just basic clean up at this point. When we get this floor cleaned, I'm going to have spa services bring down their mats so we won't keep tracking muck in again. We've got some private contractors coming in later to haul this mess away. Luckily, we're not unionized because I've got our people doing everything."

"The last of the carpeting is out." Ron Caisson, breathing heavily, came over to join them. "Morning, Dolores. What do you want done with the curtains in there, Tom?"

143

"I don't think it's worth the expense of cleaning them. Just pitch them along with the carpet. Dolores, I'm going to ask you and Brielle to take a quick inventory of what we have in the gift shop. Separate what's salvageable and what isn't. Maybe when Leon gets here, he can help carry things out to the street for you."

"Sure. Good to see you here, Ron. Did you have any trouble getting in?" Dolores asked.

"I came back last night when things started to go south."

"Wow. Long night then."

"Going to be a longer day. I'll get started on those curtains."

His assistant manager watched Ron return to where his crew was working.

"Well, that sounds promising," Dolores said, her eyes widening as she looked up at him.

"Doesn't it? He did a job and a half last night. Maybe things are beginning to turn around for him."

"How's Gentleman Jim doing with all this?"

"Actually, okay. Of course, he's seen worse in his lifetime. I mean he survived the Battle of Britain, right? The Exeter Club suffered broken pipes because of the pressure so it isn't just the ground floor that's been affected. The wainscoting there has buckled and water got into the walk-in humidor. I've scheduled a senior staff meeting up in the penthouse at ten. We all need to touch base and see where we stand."

"What's the story on the power here?" Dolores asked. "It seemed to be out most everywhere while we were driving over."

"We lost it just before midnight. We were able to

jerry-rig the emergency generator from the construction site which has been providing power for the elevators, ventilation system, and emergency lights. I left the restaurants, bars, casino areas, and kitchens in the dark. Got a ton of spoiled food now."

"Along with hungry guests."

"Right. I had an automatic phone message sent to all the rooms inviting them to use the stuff in the mini-bars to tide things over until food services can set up some kind of cold buffet."

Ron deposited a heap of draperies by the door and came over, stripping off his gloves.

"The worst of the stuff is out of Memories now, but it's going to be a while before we can re-open for business in there."

"At least it's not a critical area for operations. I just want to get the worst of this stuff out of the lobby area. Take a breather, Ron. You deserve it. I'm going to get a cart and someone from security and then we'll do the pick-ups." He turned to Dolores. "When we lost power last night, none of the receipts were collected so the shift accounting didn't get done. We need to collect the cash drawers from the bars, restaurants, casinos, and the employee tip drop boxes."

"Leon!" Dolores waved at her husband as he entered, paused and looked around, shaking his head. "Okay, Tom, Leon and I will give Brielle a hand."

Hc secured a cash cart and security guard and came back to the atrium. Outside the door he could see Ron smoking a cigarette with other employees. He parked the cart momentarily and checked his phone.

Delete, delete.

"Tom, quite a scene here."

Caught off guard, he looked up. "Joe. Didn't expect you in today. How's everything over at your place? What's Lotsa Slots look like?"

"The ground floor is a mess. Thirty years in Vegas and this tops it all. Most of our stuff was up high enough to keep it out of harm's way. Thought I'd drop by and see what the story was over here. It's Sunday. I didn't know if you wanted me to run the regular maintenance check on your machines or not," Joe Niemeyer said.

"No, no. That stuff's toxic. I haven't got anyone working over there yet. We're still trying to get the lobby area clear so we can take care of arriving and departing guests."

"Looks like you've got power. We're still waiting on it over on Fremont." The grizzled Vegas veteran shook his head.

"We were lucky to have back-up." He watched Ron stub out his cigarette, glance his way, and turn to say something to the others. "Any word on when the grid's going to be back up?"

"Someone told me maybe noon when I called in about it."

"Well, thanks for showing up, but go take care of your own place. We can probably delay maintenance on our machines for a while. Hopefully, we'll get the Imperial up and running before too long."

"Just give me a call when you need me. I have the feeling business all along Fremont is going to be down this week."

Ron rejoined him as their security guard pushed the cart into the Memories Gift Shop.

"Didn't expect to see our slots tech in today. Guess

he doesn't expect any business at his place."

"It was probably curiosity as much as anything. It's not like he doesn't have plenty to do at his store. I'm hoping at our staff meeting we can get a timeline hammered out for cleanup and restoring services. Ladies, how's it going?"

Dolores straightened up from behind a counter and rolled her eyes. "We're probably looking at a ninety percent loss here, Tom. Sweatshirts, T-shirts, calendars. You name it. Most of that stuff was down low where the surge of the water got to it. Even the plastic coverings didn't protect the merchandise."

"It wouldn't be worth the cost to sanitize it all. We'll dump it and take the write-off. Brielle, what's the story back there?"

Ron's assistant was holding the storeroom door for Leon.

"Better, the shot glasses, mugs, poker chips, and jewelry came through okay. But the stuff in boxes— playing cards, baccarat sets—all that's a loss."

Dolores rested against the wall and crossed her arms.

"It's going to take a while to re-order and restock, Tom."

"Right." He turned on the register and used his key to unlock it. "At least it's not a primary area for operations. Ron and I are making the rounds. We'll be back in accounting when we're done if you need us. Otherwise, Gentleman Jim's at ten."

"I'll be ready for a break." He heard a sigh as Dolores knelt behind the counter again.

****

He pushed the penthouse level button in Jim's

private elevator, or lift as his employer called it, and leaned back against the wall feeling his eyelids droop. Everything was catching up with him—Saturday night's deluge, the mess at the Imperial, the cold shoulder from Cinnamon, his non-accident out at Red Rock Canyon. His stomach muscles tightened as he gritted his teeth. Taking a deep breath, he pushed the anger away. He'd deal with it later. Someone would pay.

"So I guess the Imperial took the big prize last night. Brielle was all excited when she came in this morning," Ron said.

He started. "Oh, yeah, we did. Best of the small independents. Actually, I left it back at my apartment. No." He caught himself. That all seemed so long ago. "No, it's still in the Jag. I switched over to the SUV when I came back to the Imperial."

"A lot more practical. That Jag rides so low, you're practically sitting on asphalt. Brielle said everyone had a great time."

"We did until we had to go outside and deal with the weather. Saw a lot of industry people there." At least he'd thought they'd all enjoyed the evening, but what was the story with Cinna's attitude? She'd about taken his head off when he'd suggested sending help over for her from the hotel. Had he insulted her? Was she that stubbornly independent?

"You know Brielle." Ron shifted, jamming his hands into his pants' pocket. "She's been a big help around here, picking up the load."

"Dolores appreciates her."

"She's been terrific. I know I haven't been pulling my weight, Tom."

He didn't reply.

Ron lowered his head.

"Brielle's been doing her job along with most of mine, I guess. Wanda, well, since we lost R.J., she's been drinking again. I found an A.A. group that meets evenings and I think it's helping us through things. It's a special group dealing with people going through loss. Brielle has been a trooper about picking up the slack when I cut out early."

The elevator doors slid open. He waited an instant.

"I guess what I'm trying to say here, Tom, is I appreciate the opportunity. It's obvious the Imperial's a first-class place and I don't want to louse things up."

"Sure, Ron. You performed above and beyond the call of duty last night." He offered him his hand.

"Thanks. Maybe it took a storm like that to wake me up."

****

Food and Beverage had actually been able to produce a credible brunch from Gentleman Jim's kitchenette on short notice. High above the mess the downtown had turned into, sunlight poured through the penthouse's floor to ceiling windows. Dianne LaRusso had set up a tempting array of fruits, pastries, jams, flavored butters, and granola on the kitchen bar.

He bypassed the tea in favor of coffee. Fortunately, someone seemed to prefer the same full-strength caffeine he needed.

He took a seat on the couch beside Dolores who was balancing her own cup and saucer along with a platter of fresh fruit and a muffin.

"We're pretty much finished down in Memories, Chief. I left Brielle and Leon moving everything salvageable out of the way so the cleaning crews can get in and get started. The carpeting, draperies, and damaged merchandise are out in front waiting for the trash pick up."

"We're getting more accomplished than I expected. God knows when we'll be able to get new carpet laid. We'll probably have to stand in line with the other hotels." He took a long soothing sip of his coffee and mentally counted heads—Food and Beverage Services, Security, Gaming Operations, Hospitality, Special Events, Maintenance, Consumer Operations, Groundskeeping, Business Services, Housekeeping. Promotions?

"Eddie Rasmussen?"

"Eddie's out of town." Dolores dusted muffin crumbs off her manicured fingers. "Remember that conference out in Tahoe? He's due back Monday."

"Right." He dragged a hand across his face. "Excuse me. I'm fogging up here."

"Nick called in. He and Peggy are going out to see their daughter in the hospital. She had her scoliosis operation yesterday. She's doing fine, but he wants to check on her. He's going to try and make it in this afternoon."

"Good. Well then, I think we're all here."

Gentleman Jim was in his element, enjoying himself as if he were hosting an impromptu picnic. Maybe holding an occasional staff meeting in the penthouse might be a good idea in the future. Standing at the buffet table, their employer was busy pouring tea and coffee, finding silverware, and encouraging people to try a bit of this and that.

He got to his feet. "People, if we can all get our

things and find a place over here, I think we'll get started. The sooner we can get through the agenda, the sooner we can get back to work."

He waited as everyone pulled up chairs and Jim McMasters seated himself in his favorite red leather chair. His eyes bright, McMasters looked as if the events of the past twenty-four hours had energized him.

"To begin with I want to thank all of you for showing up on a Sunday. Especially to our kitchen crew currently serving a cold buffet to our guests up on the mezzanine. I know it isn't easy. I'm sure everyone here has been adversely affected by the storm last night and you all have things of your own to deal with. Your sense of commitment and work ethic were major contributors to our winning the hospitality industry award last night."

"Hear, hear!" Gentleman Jim applauded heartily. "Capital job!" He stood with the others.

"I think we'll start by going around and having everyone summarize the state of affairs in their department. We need to get an idea of where we stand and what needs to be done. Then we can prioritize the implementation of our resources and sketch out a timetable for getting back up to speed." He nodded at his secretary. "Candace, will be taking notes."

He'd need to remember and ask Candace about the status of the short sell property his secretary and her husband were negotiating to buy.

He sat back in his armchair to listen, his coffee forgotten, growing cold in his cup.

Time, money, recovery schedules. It was every bit as grim as he'd feared. How could McMasters convince his investors back in Britain to put even more money in a venture still slow to show a profit after more than three years of non-stop investment?

"But on the plus side…" Andrea Devore, head of consumer operations was persistently cheerful. If a fire alarm sounded at midnight, she'd probably wake up with a smile on her face at the thought of getting some exercise. "You know considering everything we've had very few complaints. I mean for people who spent good money expecting a sunny Las Vegas holiday, they are bearing up. Services are minimal, downstairs is a nasty swamp, and we have no idea when our restaurants and gaming areas will be back in operation. Ditto pool and spa facilities. But people have been understanding for the most part, especially those who've been with us before and know the kind of quality we're committed to."

"Good show!" McMasters said.

"It probably didn't hurt anything that we opened up the mini-bars last night," Dianne LaRusso, head of Food and Beverage, said. "Bet we'll see a lot of miniature liquor bottles in the trash today."

"Oh, but we need to do more than that for our guests!" Gentleman Jim protested. "We must compensate them for this unfortunate turn of events while the rest of us soldier on. No charge on rooms since this mess began or for our guests booking in today. No, wouldn't do at all, would it? And we'll offer a discounted rate on a future stay at the Imperial for guests affected by this sorry bit of business."

There was an awkward moment of silence. Ron and Dolores were looking at him. In the back, the door from the corridor opened and Elspeth Porter-Hayes slipped in quietly. She took a seat by the buffet table to listen. Well, he guessed it was her money they were discussing. It didn't make it any easier. He took a deep breath.

"That's a splendid idea, sir."

And it was. Just not practical in their current financial state.

"I guess I'm only worried about the bottom line." Across the room, Suresh Bindra, head of business operations, raised an eyebrow and nodded.

"Here we are, open a year now and still operating at a loss. I think we need to examine the situation from a practical standpoint."

"My dear lad, that's what insurance is for, you know. A rainy day. And that's certainly what we've had here, isn't it?"

"But that would be flood insurance," Suresh said. "Our general insurance policy is on buildings, grounds, personnel, liability. It excludes damage due to flooding."

"Oh, yes, naturally. That's the business of the National Flood Insurance Program. One must purchase a separate policy through your federal government in Washington."

Every eye in the room was focused on the Imperial's chairman.

"Which I did."

He swallowed. Had he heard correctly?

"Lord Baden-Powell, of course. I didn't spend my youth in scouting to disregard his first dictum—Be prepared. And, you know…" Gentleman Jim sounded baffled. "It was surprisingly cheap. I think they were rather surprised, you know."

For being asked to provide a flood insurance policy

on a property in a city with an average annual rainfall of four inches?

Probably.

Elspeth Porter-Hayes led the applause.

****

He and Suresh had stayed behind to discuss details with Gentleman Jim. He'd sent the rest of the staff back to work, but not before the desk had rung the penthouse suite to say full power had been restored to the downtown area.

He stood with his head of business operations at the elevator.

"You know McMasters is one in a million. If we didn't know that before, we do now," Suresh said.

"We sure do. I never considered the possibility we actually had coverage for flood damage."

A couple was coming out of one of the penthouse suites the Imperial used to comp their whales, the high rollers the casino cultivated.

"You go on," he told Suresh. "I'll be down in a minute."

"Tom!" Magdalena waved at him. She and David looked relaxed, if not entirely rested.

"Good morning. How was the suite?"

"Topping, mate, wizard. Believe me, I've seen enough of the other kind knocking about as I do."

Mate, topping, knocking about. Brit speak. Thanks to Gentleman Jim, he didn't need a translator.

"Glad you could use it. Without service to or from the airport, it was just going to waste. And it was the least we could do for your help in getting the generator up and running last night. You saved our bacon. "

"Bacon." David sounded mystified. "Ah, yes,

refrigeration woes. Well, one does pick up the odd lot of skills in my line of work."

"I saw Cinna this morning. I stopped in at the shop to see how everything was, but she seemed to have things under control." Or was desperate to give that impression. Was it her pride that had caused the frostiness even Rosemary and her boyfriend seemed to have noticed? Had his offer offended her?

Magdalena looked at David and made a face. "Poor Cinna. She must be going nuts wondering where I am, leaving her alone to cope with everything."

"Actually, her sister and a friend were over there when I stopped by."

"Rosemary? I knew they were in town. Cinna had lunch with them on the Strip the other day."

"Rosemary was going to stay and help out for a while. Her boyfriend walked back here with me to see some of the flood damage and I gave him an abbreviated tour."

"We've been watching the news coverage online. It looks like a sodding disaster out there," David said.

"I don't know when we'll be back to normal." Tom pressed the elevator button for them. "Most of the day shift showed up today, but everything's at six and sevens. I've got blackjack dealers and croupiers ripping out carpeting, bartenders and wait staff carrying out trash, spa attendants power washing walls. Everyone who depends on tips is going to be hurting for a while."

"I'll be glad when we're back in business. Cinna and I may be living out of our tip jar for a while." Magdalena grimaced and looked up at David.

"Tips. Your gratuities. I always have to remind myself they're not included in the bill here in the

States."

"Sometimes I feel like the quarter queen of north Vegas. But even change adds up to real money."

Tips. Real money. Change. Was there some connection there he should be seeing? The elevator door had opened. He remained where he was, frozen in thought. David and Magdalena were waiting on him.

"No, go on down." He shook his head. "I think there are some things I need to check on."

Chapter Twelve

Don Dennis bent forward, frowning as he examined the strands of the frayed rope. His chief of security had set up a temporary office on the mezzanine. Sitting up, he gripped an unbroken section of the rope and pulled on it. Letting out a low whistle, he looked up at him.

"And this happened when you were rock climbing out at Red Rock Canyon?"

"Yeah." He shifted carefully in his chair. "In a section I've climbed a number of times although I picked a shorter way up this time. I wanted to be sure I'd have enough time to be back for the awards banquet at the convention center."

"Well, there isn't a thing wrong with this intact section of rope. No reason for it to give way, except it's been tampered with."

"That's what I thought." He took the rope back from Don, coiled it, and replaced it in his briefcase. "From what I can tell, only the interior strands were cut so it wasn't apparent something was wrong until it had to support my weight."

"So how high up were you?"

"Not too far. Couple hundred feet, maybe."

"Enough to do a lot of damage." Taking a toothpick from his jacket pocket, Don inserted it in his mouth and leaned back in his chair.

"Yeah, well, I don't know if someone was trying to kill me or just put me out of action for a while."

"Tom, if you'd fallen down that rock face, I'd say they really didn't care one way or the other."

"Probably not."

"When was the last time you used your equipment?"

"I can't be sure. I'd guess it's been six weeks. Maybe more."

"And it's been stored in your room here."

"Right. I checked it over when I returned after my last trip and again before I started out Saturday, but it looked fine to me." He shook his head.

"It's not easy to clip the interior strands and not disturb the outside. My guess is the weapon of choice was probably a pair of manicure scissors. Six weeks is a big window for someone to sabotage your stuff. Security and housekeepers carry entry cards to all our rooms. My people keep possession of theirs. Housekeepers are supposed to turn theirs in when they finish their shift. Their pay is docked if they don't. Senior staff has access to them at the front desk." He raised an eyebrow.

"You got any ideas?"

"Maybe. I think some things are starting to fall into place."

"You want me to put in a call to the LVPD? This kind of thing is out of my bailiwick."

"Eventually, yeah, I want the police to look into it, but besides having to deal with the flood aftermath here, there's something I'd like to check out first."

"More important than attempted murder?"

"Maybe connected to it. Care to come up with me

to the eye in the sky office? I need to look at some surveillance tape."

"Glad to." Don pushed his chair back and pitched his toothpick in a wastepaper basket.

"Lead on, Tom."

****

Roxane Cox was by sitting by herself in front of the wall of monitors as they entered. She turned to look at them. He waited, as Don closed the door, for his eyes to adjust to the low lights.

"Everything's quiet here. No surprises," Roxane said. "Terrance called in a while ago. He's stuck at his place with a flooded-out car. I told him I could cover things today."

"Yeah, I'm not expecting much action." He moved over to stand beside Roxane. The bank of monitors provided clear pictures of Ron supervising clean up on the first floor, elevators moving guests, along with sweeps of the deserted casinos, bars, and restaurants.

"Any problems, Tom?" Roxane asked.

He shook his head.

"What kind of surveillance do we have when areas are shut down for housekeeping and maintenance?" He pointed at a screen. "Like when housekeeping comes in to clean the baccarat room."

"Well, they clean during off hours so probably no one's really watching too closely," Roxane said slowly. "The cameras roll on a continuous loop so we can always replay the footage if we have a question about something. Is there a problem?"

"I don't know. I'm not quite sure what I'm looking for. Can you pull up surveillance on the slots room for me?"

"Right here." Roxane pointed to a screen. "Looks like cleanup hasn't made it in yet. I can give you the whole room or," she tapped some keys on her keyboard, "I can zoom in for close-up. Do you want anything in particular?"

He shook his head. It was just as he remembered it. The camera angle was positioned behind the customers. The eye in the sky was focused on their play and the fronts of the machines.

He straightened up. Was that part of the problem?

"Don, I'd like you to find Ron and meet me down at Slotz! in about fifteen minutes. Tell Ron to bring a tool kit along."

"Sure, Tom, I'll track him down."

"Thanks, and Don, let's keep this on the Q.T. please."

His security chief nodded and left the room. Over his years in Vegas, he'd probably had any number of strange requests.

Roxane looked at him and went back to watching her monitors.

He knew he was being mysterious, but it was hard to explain what you didn't understand yourself. He was on the wildest of goose chases.

He let himself out and found his phone. Cell phone transmissions were back up. A month ago, he'd programmed SpecialTeas' number into his cell.

Cinna sounded past exhaustion when she answered.

"Cinna, this is Tom. Please just one quick question." He rushed past any attempt for her to get a word in.

"Tell me this. The other day you said something about having seen the Imperial's chips, noticing how

160

different they were. I need to know, where was it you ran across them?"

****

"Well, hello, Sleeping Beauty." Magdalena was on the couch in her nightshirt. She found the remote and turned down the sound on the television. "I was beginning to wonder how long you were going to be in the shower."

"Sorry to be hogging it." Cinna took a seat on the arm of the couch, toweling off her damp hair.

"Hey, no problem. When I got in last night, you were still in your clothes, dead to the world. I apologize for sticking you with the heavy lifting. David and I spent Saturday night at the Imperial. Then he brought me back here to change and we went out to eat. Boy, is this area a disaster zone or what? We ended up down on the Strip. By the time I got back to the shop, you had left. Looks like you got quite a bit done."

"Rosemary helped. She and her boyfriend stopped by. They were curious about damage downtown. I wish she could have seen the shop before the flood hit."

"Yeah. Tom said they were there when he stopped in. We ran into him as we were leaving."

Cinna wrapped her towel around her hair and shuddered.

"Cut the man some slack, girl. He was super nice to David and me, treating us to dinner at the Imperial and then giving us a suite when the deluge started."

"You stayed overnight there?"

"A-l-l night." Magdalena drew out the word and stretched luxuriously.

"You and…"

"Me and our visitor from the land of Kama Sutra.

161

I'll tell you I gave him something to think about on those lonely hikes though the Himalayan foothills thumbing his way from one tea plantation to another. And that suite!" Magdalena wiggled her hips down into the sofa and lay back staring at the ceiling.

"Three huge rooms, Cinna, whirlpool tub, floor to ceiling windows, a black leather sofa like butter. You could spend the rest of your life on it and not complain. Especially if you had company." She giggled. "A fully stocked kitchen, surround sound, silk duvet. It, well, let's just say it was a night to remember." She sat up, raising her mug in salute. "Want some tea?"

Cinna shook her head, staring at the floor.

"Cinna?" Magdalena leaned closer. "What's wrong? Are you crying?"

She swallowed, started to say something and stopped.

"You are." Magdalena reached out a hand to touch her cheek. "What's the matter, baby?"

"Oh, just everything." She ran a finger under her eyes. "Everything's screwed up. My whole messy life. The store. Tom. I hate him."

"What happened?"

"I spent the night with him, Mags."

"Saturday night?"

She nodded. "Only I didn't mean to." Her chest heaved. "I didn't. I really didn't. It was that horrible harmony tea. And the storm. And maybe that damned, damned tuxedo."

"What do you mean? Tell me what's going on." Magdalena reached for a tissue from the box on the coffee table and passed it to her. "Sit down, honey. What's going on?" She reached for a tissue from the box on the coffee table and passed it to her.

"He took me to his apartment after the dinner." She crumpled the tissue in her hand. "He said it was raining so hard that he didn't know if he could get downtown. I took a shower to get warm and when I came into the bedroom, he'd left a cup of tea there. Later he came in and…you know. Mags, he and I spent the night together." Her body shook. "I couldn't, I just couldn't resist him. And oh." She looked up and wiped her nose with the tissue. "Even if he wasn't the father of Rosemary's child back in Des Moines, he shouldn't have…n-not when I was so out of it. I didn't know what was going on." She put her head down into her hands.

"Rosemary had a baby?"

"Yeah, but it turned out it wasn't Tom's. It was some lowlife ex-teacher of ours she got involved with after she and Tom broke up. She put the baby up for adoption."

"And you think you and Tom spent Saturday night together after the awards banquet." Magdalena sounded mystified.

"Um." Cinna bobbed her head. "Yes, I'm sorry about it, but yes."

"No, Cinna, you didn't," Magdalena said carefully.

Cinna looked at her.

"What time did you leave the convention center?"

"It was about eleven, I think."

"Okay." Magdalena bit her lip. "He drove you back through the rain to his apartment. Then you took a shower, went to the bedroom, drank the tea, and he came in."

"Yes. I think it was that horrible celestial harmony tea we came up with. He used it and…" She used the

163

fresh tissue Magdalena passed her, her shoulders shaking.

"But that can't be, Cinna. The times don't work. Tom spent the night at the Imperial."

"What do you mean?"

"David and I had dinner at the Reserve, their penthouse restaurant. It was wonderful. We took our time. Sometime after eleven the area lost power. Everyone just stood by the windows watching the lightning storm over Vegas. I never saw anything like it. Lightning was arcing from one horizon to the other. There were these huge booms of thunder and transformers exploding like fireworks. You get a 360-degree view from up there. The kitchen staff came out and started pouring drinks for everyone. It wasn't like they could do a lot else.

"Anyway, around midnight Tom came up with a guy named Ron. They had climbed the stairs checking on things. They came over to where we were. Tom talked about winning the award and said you were staying at his place for the night."

Cinna stared at her.

"So he wasn't with you. He couldn't have been. He and Ron talked about utilizing the construction equipment in some part of the hotel property that's under development. Ron thought there was an emergency generator down there. David is pretty much of a jack-of-all-trades and he offered to help them with it. Anyway about two or three o'clock, they got it hooked up and turned on. Then Tom put David and me up in one of their high roller suites. So…" She moistened her lips and looked at Cinna.

"Tom didn't have time to take you from the

convention center to his place, fix tea for you, wait 'til you got out of the shower, seduce you, change clothes, make it over to the Imperial, climb fourteen flights of stairs, and get to the Reserve by midnight." Magdalena shook her head. "It doesn't make sense."

"But I remember it." Every hard, strong line of Tom's body was etched in her memory. The way her own had responded.

"Cinna, he didn't go back to his apartment later either. When we were leaving the Imperial Sunday, we ran into Ron in the lobby. He talked to David and me about how he and Tom had worked on things there all through the night, about getting their pumps going." She waited in silence a minute.

"Are you sure it wasn't a wild dream you had? I mean like him or not, you've got to admit he is damned good-looking. How much did you have to drink at the dinner, honey?"

"Not that much. Barely anything. One glass of wine before dinner and then later a glass of champagne when they won their award. Oh, and a couple sips from another glass just before we left." When she had picked up Tom's unused champagne glass.

"Well, I don't know, kid." Magdalena cocked her head and looked at her. "How do you feel?" She raised her eyebrows.

Cinna drew a shaky breath. "Tired, wiped out."

"But not sore, shall we say?"

"No." She drew the word out. "Not that way."

"Okay. So maybe it was the combination of the storm, being around magnificent Marco, the alcohol you did have." Magdalena shrugged and reached for her mug again. "Whatever. But I do believe my night was better than yours."

****

There seemed to be an urgency to Joe Niemeyer's step as he hurried out of Slotz! tool box in hand.

From his position in the corner, Tom nodded to Ron. His day shift supervisor had been ready for action since their meeting the night before with Gentleman Jim. The two of them walked briskly across the floor on an intercept course, his security team following behind.

"Wait up, Joe," he called.

The other man whirled around and started as if his mind had been on other things.

Don Dennis and Hussein Ahmed took hold of Joe's upper arms in their practiced professional way.

"We're going to ask you to accompany us, Mr. Niemeyer," Don said.

"What the hell? What's going on here?" Joe's head swiveled from the Imperial's chief of security to his deputy.

"We're going to take a walk over to the business office. We need to take a look at some things." Tom nodded at his security officers who began moving quietly, their reluctant guest in tow.

"You can't—"

"Actually, we can." Ron's voice rang with confidence. "If you check the State of Nevada Revised Statute 465, you'll see it grants casinos the authority to detain suspects on suspicion of cheating."

"What? Cheating? What are you talking… Hey!"

It only took a minute to navigate the back hallway to the accounting office. Between Ron, Gentleman Jim, and him last night, they had come up with a plan designed to avoid notice as much as possible.

The counting room was secure; few casino employees were allowed to enter. In hindsight, perhaps, the limited approved list had been one of the problems.

Joe seemed more than ready to sit when Hussein and Don got him to a chair as though his legs couldn't be depended on.

"Okay, let's see what we've got." Tom nodded to Ron as he placed Joe's toolbox on the table in front of him. The Lotsa Slots owner stared at it as if he didn't recognize it, swallowing convulsively as Ron popped the latch. Under the overhead lights, Joe's forehead gleamed.

The top drawers held a variety of miniature tools— screwdrivers, timers, wrenches, calibrators, and spanners. Ron lifted out the drawer to reveal cleaning rags and several plastic bags. He held up one containing small metal bars.

He nodded. They'd seen one of them last night.

"I don't know wha…" Joe's voice trailed away as Ron used the tip of a screwdriver to raise the bottom of the box.

"Well, look here. What do you think, boss?" Ron didn't sound surprised.

"Okay, Don and Hussein, I'll need you to verify that we have found Joe Niemeyer in possession of a number of Imperial Casino chips concealed in the false bottom of his tool box."

"So I-I like to gamble a little." Joe attempted a shrug. "Who doesn't? This is Vegas, guys."

Don Dennis was doing a quick count.

"Except employees are not permitted to gamble on company property which, as a contracted service technician, includes you. And you didn't get these by

167

gambling," Don said.

"Eighteen hundred, Tom. Including…" He held a chip up.

"As the four of us will testify, we pulled the back off a slot machine last night. Imagine what we found in the bottom. Including one chip we shaved the edge on. Interesting little set-up with the magnets."

Joe licked his lips and stared at the table.

"I want a lawyer," he mumbled.

"Right. Well, I'm going to put in a call to gaming control." He looked over at Ron. "Hussein and I will stay here with Joe if you and Don want to head up to the front desk and finish the rest of this business."

"My pleasure," Ron said. "Been looking forward to it." He was already at the door.

****

There was root beer and ginger ale in the refrigerator along with bottled water but he didn't know if he could make it that far. It was a good twelve, fifteen feet from the sofa plus the distance back. It seemed better to stay where he was, muscles molding themselves into the sofa back, gravity pushing down, eyelids relaxing.

He wasn't sure if he'd heard a knock on the door or if he'd imagined it.

It came again, slight, tentative, as if unsure. *What the?* With his irregular schedule, he didn't get many visitors. And he didn't know any of his neighbors since the friendly older lady down the hall had been evicted for the interesting collection of houseplants under a grow light the apartment cleaning service had found.

He pushed himself up to his feet, wincing a little. Still sore, he held his chest and got the knob.

"Cinna?" He blinked. A figure was turning away.

"Oh, Tom." Cinnamon was dressed in a sleeveless shift, arms and legs bare, her heavy blonde curls secured with a barrette.

"I'm sorry to bother you, I can see you're tired. This is probably a bad time with everything going on."

He drug a hand over his face. Did he look as bad as he felt? The last few days must be showing.

"Please come in. It's fine. I just got home a little while ago. I've been laying around."

"I'm sorry. Things must still be a mess at the hotel. Dolores said you'd be here." She passed him, trailing a scent of girl stuff. Shampoo? Soap? Cinna? He closed his eyes and drank it in.

"I'm just…" She swallowed. "I wanted to come by to apologize. And to thank you. Magdalena, Mags told me how you put her and David up Saturday."

"It was the least I could do. Please have a seat." She looked uneasy. What was going on? She sat down on the edge of the couch, avoiding his gaze, twisting her fingers in her lap.

"It was the least I could do," he repeated. "Between David, Ron, and me, the three of us got the emergency generator up and going and enough power for essential services. The whole downtown area blacked out around midnight."

"That's what Magdalena said. They were at the Reserve having dinner when it happened."

"We were lucky to have the generator available at the construction site. Witheroe's done a bit of everything in his travels. Ron and I provided the unskilled labor. Dave is an expert on more things than tea."

She looked at the floor, not quite repressing a shiver.

A topic to avoid? What was going on? With Cinnamon, there seemed to be land mines he couldn't anticipate. He cleared his throat. It seemed he needed to change the subject.

"Well, we solved one mystery today at the Imperial."

"What's that?" She raised her head to look at him. There were shadows under her eyes.

"We've been losing money. Not a lot, but a steady drain we couldn't explain. It was enough to keep us in the red and our investors unhappy. You remember the question I called up to ask you?"

"And I almost bit your head off."

"Right." He raised an eyebrow. "I wanted to know where it was that you first saw chips from our casino."

"And I told you one time when I was making a delivery at Lotsa Slots."

"You had mentioned Joe Niemeyer being a steady customer of yours. How he started his Monday mornings with a double Darjeeling and almond biscotti."

"You have a good memory."

About you, oh, yes.

"But you hadn't been in the Imperial yet when you mentioned our chips. That was before your trip over when you met Gentleman Jim. Why would you see our chips out somewhere, off casino property? Chips aren't legal tender anywhere except in the casino that issues them. I was curious about where you'd run across them."

She shrugged her shoulders. "Joe had them out on

his counter one morning when I stopped in with his order. They caught my eye because they were so different. I mean I know the colors are always the same in every casino. The one dollar chips are always white and fives are red and so on, but yours were stamped with the St. George's cross on the back of one, St. Andrew's on another, the Union Jack on something. They were distinctive, but I didn't think any more about them."

"No, but Imperial employees aren't permitted to gamble on our premises and, as one of our contracted technicians, that includes Niemeyer. It raised a question about how he got them. Had someone passed them to him, or had he obtained them illegally?"

"Illegally? From the slot machines?"

"He showed up Sunday morning to service the machines. It was his regular time, but it seemed odd that he'd come in when we were hip deep in cleaning up from a flood. Servicing the slots was the last thing on my agenda. I sent him home and got to wondering about it. It wasn't like he didn't have other things to do. Anyway, Ron and I pulled the back off one of the machines yesterday afternoon to take a look at it."

"Was it rigged?"

"Big time. Joe had installed a small weak magnet. Just enough to hold the opening open a second longer when someone hit a jackpot. The jackpots aren't progressive. They pay fixed amounts. When one hits, the chips fall down into the cup for the player. Except with Joe's magnet holding the chip dispenser open a second longer, an extra chip would fall down the back of the machine after the opening to the hopper closed and our service technician would get a nice payoff every Sunday when he came in to service the slots."

"And he'd take the chips back to his store."

"Concealed in his toolbox. But he still had the problem of cashing them. As an Imperial employee, he didn't dare do it himself and attract attention. It was your friend Magdalena who clued me in to what was happening."

"What do you mean?"

"I ran into her and David as they were leaving the Imperial yesterday. She said something about having to live off tip money until you two could reopen. How tip money added up to real money."

"Okay?"

"Casino chips are legal tender only in our gaming venues. They can't be used in the restaurants, bars, gift shop, or anywhere else. But guests do tip the dealers with them. Most players leave a tip when they stop playing a game. It can be cash or chips, but everything goes into a drop box that's collected at the end of a shift. The boxes are collected and taken to a count room for accounting. Dealers share tips based on amount of hours they work."

He rubbed the back of his neck. He and Ron had outlined the scam to Gentleman Jim in his penthouse last night as the older man had sat transfixed, scarcely breathing.

"The totals are entered into the computer. It's a good part of the compensation our employees work for. Two supervisors are supposed to be present whenever money is counted."

"Supposed to."

"Yeah." He leaned forward. "I always thought it odd the way Brielle stuck up for Ron. It bugged me that she didn't seem to resent the extra work he was sticking her with. She never campaigned for his job or tried to get him fired. And, believe me, that would have been a possibility. No, she was always willing to fill in for him when he cut out early or was unavailable to do something."

She nodded.

"We all know Ron's been dealing with a lot—the loss of his son, problems in his marriage, and the fact he didn't get the job he thought he ought to. He assumed when the Imperial reopened he would be assistant manager like he had been at the Outpost. Only Dolores, who'd been head of housekeeping somewhere else, was clearly the superior candidate. About a month ago, I blew up during a staff meeting and really landed on him. He'd been letting a lot of things slide." That had been right after the last time he'd gone rock climbing, then stored his equipment in his room at the Imperial.

"I should have handled the situation privately. I did apologize to Ron when I cooled off. But Brielle always stuck up for him. She didn't want him fired and us bringing someone else in to take his place. She was using the situation. If I were discredited or injured and out of action, it would keep their scam going. She'd pick up the chips from Niemeyer and switch them out for cash from the tip drop boxes when Ron cut out early and she did the accounting by herself.

"She even knew enough about where the camera in the count room was located that she could casually block the angle of coverage. The tallies always looked problem free and she could manipulate the chip totals in the machines so we didn't catch on that the machines were paying off in excess as to what they should."

"I can't believe it. She seemed so quiet, kind of shy."

"Everyone thought she was great. She had her own cheering section. I think that was part of the racket they were working. Together, they could bleed off a couple thousand a week as long as Ron wasn't hanging around to supervise the count. I put in a call to Joe last night to come over to service the machines today. We caught him leaving, chips concealed in his toolbox. Right now, he and Brielle are down at headquarters in a race to rat each other out."

"She seemed familiar to me. Maybe I ran into her at Lotsa Slots."

He stretched and grimaced. "It's been a long couple days."

"I didn't make it any easier on you, did I?"

"What's going on, Cinna? I stepped into something when I stopped by the shop yesterday. I thought things went well Saturday night. Except for the part where the heavens opened and we almost drowned."

"I had some questions. I have some questions, Tom, about Saturday night. About the tea you made me. And what happened afterward." Her voice shook.

"Tea?" Where the hell was that coming from? He stared at her.

"You know, the cup you left on the bedside table while I was in the shower."

So it wasn't up to her specifications?

"I thought you could use something warm to drink after being out in that mess."

She took a breath, lifted her chin, and looked at him squarely. "So what was it? Did you use our leftover

174

Celestial Harmony blend?"

"What?"

"You know, the tea from our shop that caused all the problems during the darts tournament."

"What? No, Cinna."

"Well, it tasted strange."

"It was just out of my kitchen. I used a regular teabag and the microwave."

"The microwave!" Her voice rose. "You used a regular teabag and the microwave?"

Hell, what was she mad about?

"It was some I bought when I wanted iced tea last summer. It was from the grocery store. Cinna, I don't need any help to seduce you."

Her eyes widened. Good, that was the reaction he wanted to see.

"It was just ordinary supermarket tea, the kind that comes in the box with the old sea captain on it. Did you think or feel different afterward?"

"I thought." She took a deep breath and began again. "I was so groggy when I woke up and I thought, well, that something had happened with us. Between us, you know. I had really wild dreams about you that I thought were real. But then Mags told me you were at the Imperial that night."

"I left a note on the kitchen counter to say I was going over to the Imperial to check on things. Then I swapped the Jag for my SUV and made it through."

"I didn't see the note. Everything felt strange when I woke up Sunday morning. I just grabbed my things and got out of there."

He leaned forward, elbows on his knees.

"You were confused when you woke up? Felt

different than usual?"

"Totally different. I was groggy, disoriented. I couldn't think clearly. It was like I was hung over, but I really hadn't had that much to drink."

Yeah, drinking. He paused to think.

"Do you remember what you did just before we left the convention center? When you got up to go? You reached over—"

"And took a sip of champagne from your glass, right. I'd already finished mine."

"It was still full because I don't drink. And Brielle had moved over to sit beside you when Dolores and I went up to get the award. I saw her when we were walking back."

"You think she put something in your drink, Tom? That she tried to drug you?"

"She was definitely interested in getting me in trouble or out of the way." He flexed his hands. "I need to talk to the police about it."

"Oh, God." She slumped forward, resting her head in her hands for a long instant before sitting up. "There's something else I've been blaming you for, too." She made a face. "Rosemary had a baby after you two broke up."

"She did?" His head jerked. "Cinna, it wasn't mine."

"I know. She just told me yesterday when I got on her about being friendly to you. I couldn't understand her being nice to you after how you'd treated her. I thought you had run off and left her."

"It wasn't about that."

"She told me she'd fallen for you, but then she realized it was our family that was the real attraction for you. Her pride was hurt and she got involved with some creepy ex-teacher of ours. Anyway, she put the baby up for adoption and got on with her life. She's actually in a pretty good place now. I think Ed might be the guy for her."

"It wasn't your family, as nice as they were, Cinna." The room was growing dark, faint streetlight filtering in through the blinds. "I had to make up something, some excuse. At a real awkward time, I came out with your name. It was hard to explain why I was calling someone on the verge of giving herself to me by her kid sister's name. I'm not sure what I said." He gave a quick smile. "Probably something as stupid as the way I asked you for a date last week."

"Me?"

"Always, Cinna. I couldn't very well tell the terrific girl I was dating I was hung up on her teenaged sister, that I wanted her in the worse way.

"I still do, Cinnamon."

"I just…" Her voice trailed off before she drew a deep breath. "I had a puppy love crush on you back then. I thought you were honest and nice and smart and funny and then you left. I was so angry. It seems like I've been angry ever since."

He stood, pulling his shirt out and unbuttoning it, letting it fall open. She stared at his chest.

"Your dreams the other night, did they include this?"

His chest gleamed white in the light from the street; the emergency room bandages securely wrapped around it from his waist upward.

She looked at him mutely.

"A little souvenir from a fall I took rock-climbing

177

Saturday. There was a problem with my equipment. Halfway up, the rope I was using gave way. The inside strands had been cut. Fortunately, I was able to swing myself onto a rock ledge and wait there for rescue. A couple park rangers climbed up to where I was and stabilized me enough so I could get down and be taken to the E.R."

"Oh, God, Tom." He captured her fingers in his as she held out her hand.

"It's just a couple cracked ribs. Believe me, I've had worse. My rope is in the possession of the LVPD now, and hopefully, they can use it to sweat the truth out of Miss Brielle Bennett. My climbing equipment was stored in a room here so there are a limited number of people who had access to it.

"But now, Cinnamon." He drew her up to face him. Except for the streetlight outside, the room was dark.

"Tell me about your dreams," he ordered.

"I was naked," she said. "That robe I'd put on was laying on the floor."

He caught his breath.

She reached behind her. There was the sound of a zipper descending as her dress cascaded to the floor, followed by her bra. Her breasts were white mounds in the dimness.

"Completely?"

She kicked her sandals off and slid her underpants down. She stood to release her tumble of hair, tossing the barrette on the couch.

"Oh, Cinnamon." He undid his pants, pushed his shorts down, and sat.

"Oh, Cinnamon." He caught her hand and pulled her in, straddling her legs over the arms of the chair and onto him. He cupped her face in his hands and said the last coherent words he could manage.

"I'm so sorry, my darling. I love you and I can't wait."

****

She gasped, burying her head in his neck as he pulled her in, lowering her as her legs parted. She had thought after all those years she was ready for him, but that confidence disappeared in the strength of his thrust as he entered her, wrapping his arms around her, pressing her down as he filled her.

She'd never had sex like this. She was lost. Captured, swept away in sensations, unable, unwilling to escape. She was drowning, abandoning all sense of who she was, screaming for release and breathless simultaneously.

It continued. On and on past enduring. What was she but some naked body desperate for deliverance? Her fingers dug in his shoulders as she moved with him working for satisfaction. She had to find it before she shattered into pieces.

She came first, her head sagging against him, damp with sweat as he possessed her. Then he was quiet, his chest heaving under its bandages, his hands traveling slowly, caressing their way down her back.

Some time later, she was roused out of her stupor enough to realize he was carrying her into the bedroom, undressing, and lying down beside her, covering her with kisses and pulling her to him where she belonged.

Chapter Thirteen

She woke up to find him lying on his side, propped up on an elbow, watching her, heavy lids shading his hazel eyes.

"Good morning."

"Hi." She wiggled under the tangled sheet, bare skin against the cotton.

"Here." He reached over to free her. "Okay? So how did you sleep?" He pulled a curl out from behind her ear and traced a line down her cheek.

"Oh, great, well, you know." She stretched, her nipples teasing the top of the sheet.

"Better than your first night here?"

"Much better." Then she had awoken half-drugged with whatever Brielle had slipped into the champagne, heartsick about what she thought Tom had done.

His fingers found her lips, playing with her full lower one.

"Tom."

"Cinnamon." He planted a lazy kiss on her shoulder bone.

"We need to talk about last night. We ah…weren't exactly careful, you know."

"No." He straightened back up. "I don't think the word careful has anything to do with what happened."

"We didn't take any precautions. I'm not on the pill or anything."

"And you think you might be expecting our first?"

"It's a possibility, isn't it? I'm not sure exactly what time of the month it is for me." She wrinkled her brow. "Although it may be a little late to worry about that now."

"Well, fortunately, we live in the quickie marriage capital of the U.S. Do you think Fred and Ginger would have trouble with the idea of becoming grandparents if I knocked up their younger daughter?"

"Tom, be serious. We're talking about a baby here. A potential baby." She pulled the sheet up to her neck.

"Our baby, Cinna." His eyes were intense, the green glint back. "C'mon now, we're old enough. I'm thirty-five and you're what? Thirty? Don't you think it's time two people in love got started on the important things in life?"

She swallowed as he moved over her, his face inches away.

"I've got protection in the bathroom." He nodded toward the door. "Say the word and I'll get it, but I've got to tell you, Cinnamon, you've got about five seconds to decide."

She didn't waste his time.

A word about the author...

Nina Barrett's desire to be a writer began in childhood when she fell in love with words, treasuring the works of authors such as Mary Stewart and Daphne du Maurier. She is the author of two previously published novels, *Marriage Made in Haven* and *Return of the Dixie Deb*. She is an advocate for research into autism.